Don't Tell A Soul
A Mark St. James Novel

Nicolae Andrews

Cadmus Publishing
www.cadmuspublishing.com

Copyright © 2022 Nicolae Andrews

Published by Cadmus Publishing
www.cadmuspublishing.com
Port Angeles, WA

ISBN: 978-1-63751-304-0

FOR STELLA

TABLE OF CONTENTS

Prologue

The Surgeon

Tuesday, May 9, 2006
9:28 p.m.

The man stalked the night streets the way a coyote searches for prey in the wilderness. He was a most unlikely predator, but a predator nonetheless. Moving silently down Main, no one would have a second thought in passing him. He was too plain looking; at least, this is how he wished everyone to see him. The Surgeon was very light footed despite his size. Being an ex-Navy S.E.A.L., he had broad shoulders and an athletic build. His brown eyes appeared almost black without direct light on them. The night suited him well, and almost seemed consumed by his ebony skin.

This was the third of several reconnaissance missions he was doing. The man was looking for any flaws in his plan. So far, he'd seen several, but all of them were easily overcome. The woods behind the establishment would serve as an excellent entry and exit point. The main problem was the windows. This was his only real excuse for not executing the job yet. In the end The

Surgeon knew he would complete the mission; it was his duty of course. He'd been contracted, and never since his training days had he ever failed a job or accepted one he thought he couldn't complete. Nowadays all his jobs presented challenges. Adapt and overcome. Adapt and overcome. This was and had always been his mission guideline.

Stepping into the shadows near the hospital's parking area, he studied the objective. He no longer questioned the morality of the objectives in any mission he undertook. It always came down to duty and honor. When he made a decision, it was final; therefore, all jobs he accepted were done from duty and honor.

Once again, he found himself reflecting back on the day of his first kill . . .

Kirkuk, Iraq 1996

He was meant to heal, not kill. His skills were designed for life, not death. Today the tools of his craft had blood on them, stained with finality. They no longer felt the same to him. Overpowered by the guilt of what had just happened, he fell to his knees.

His comrade in arms patted his shoulder and muttered, "It was you or him man, you done nothing wrong," and then with more strength in his voice, "This is war, he'd have killed you without mercy." Squeezing his shoulder, he said, "You done your duty, that's all man!"

Still overwhelmed with guilt, he stood up . . .

Shaking his head as if to erase unwanted memories, he returned his thoughts to the present day. He'd already memorized the layout of the building. He knew how many exits there were, where all the furniture was set up, the lights, even where and how all the vents were placed. He knew how many were expected to be at work, as well as how many additional people were normally there. All of these things he knew after the first hour of studying the documents provided for the mission. It came second hand to him.

While considering all of this, the final decision was made. He regretted this decision only because it would give him less time with the victims. Duty overcame pleasure—always. This was his first rule. He figured just the adrenaline of this new mission would overcome the regret, though.

Continuing down Main he took notice of the Catholic church before taking a right on Second. If anyone had seen him when he had glanced at the church, they would have seen one of his few emotional responses. His face held a clear look of contempt. He despised all forms of religion, but especially Christianity. Religion was for fools and hypocrites.

Briefly halting toward the end of the block, he looked at the tavern as he contemplated going in. It was a large establishment, definitely an older building, remodeled several times over. It appeared the original mason had designed an all-brick building, made up of red and black with discolored glass bricks periodically placed about five feet high instead of windows. There were three steel vents for ventilation, slats facing down to keep rainwater from getting inside. The name of the tavern had been clearly remodeled several times. 'The Wagonwheel' was done all in tiles with an actual small wooden wheel for the 'o' in the word. The sign was illuminated by a long fluorescent light below the title, with a short clear plastic overhang to weatherproof it.

He knew he was a stranger to this town, and the less people saw him the easier the job would be. Being seen would add to the risk of being caught, especially with this job. It always came down to duty—he moved on. The adrenaline and killing were very pleasing, but he didn't want to get caught. It was the risk which brought enjoyment.

Stopping at 308 Second Street, he walked up the driveway, opened the gate with his pocketknife, and entered the residence's backyard. Going directly to the back door, he walked into the kitchen. Upon entering, he paused at the sight of the man sitting on the bar stool leaning against the island.

The man said, "How close are you to beginning?"

The Surgeon looked at the well-groomed man's face. "Another day is all I will need for preparation." Then, with more than a hint of disgust, "What do you gain from this, and why the symbol?"

The man, who he knew only as Chicanery, responded, "What I gain is my business. As for the symbol, let's just say I'm sending a message. You have already been given the rest of the information you need. Any further questions can be answered by remembering who I am and how much I'm paying you. Just don't screw up, and keep me informed on the schedule."

With as much sarcasm as he could muster, he muttered, "Yes, sir!"

Leaving the man in the kitchen, he walked through the atrium, past the dining room, and opened the basement door. Going down the stairs into the wine cellar, he walked toward the east wall. As he lifted a bottle of 1776 White Merlot wine from its rack, a section of the wall began to break loose and open inward, then to the right on its track. As he walked through into the hidden, well-furnished room, the door began closing.

The hand-made storm shelter was about 20 by 25 feet long, and was fully equipped with electricity, ventilation, and restroom facilities. While cramped, it was elaborately done and since its use was minimal, satisfactory. In the northeast corner were the toilet and shower area, which occasionally doubled as a place to dissect someone's body. Even this knowledge did not bother The Surgeon, since he was accustomed to death in all manners and forms. Separated by a small partitioned wall and curtain, the meager kitchen/dining utilities were on the northwest wall. These were practically brand-new items because they were only used when visitors such as himself were living in this shelter.

The rest of the room contained a bed, dresser, end table, LA-Z-BOY, and a TV with full DVD capabilities. Sound was not an issue, due to the room being built with sound proofing walls and without any windows. It was a very private room. The only remarkable thing was how such a compact area had limitless potential for the many dead bodies which had come through the room.

Nevertheless, the man was disgusted with the space he had been provided. He despised being degraded by the status this room relegated him to. The man upstairs may be a highly intelligent, educated killer but to him the man was nothing more than another disrespectful, white trash, inbred. He had to keep a tight leash on his emotions, though. A job was a job, and following his second rule, 'Duty comes before emotion,' was just as important as the first. Rules were what had allowed him to not only complete all of his missions, but also remain free to do more.

Taking a deep breath, he moved to the end of the bed and began his nightly exercises. Removing his shirt, revealing toned abs and a long scar running from his upper chest to the right side of his belly button, he dropped to the floor and began counting out 250 military-style push-ups. Becoming lost in his exercise routine, his mind returned to reflecting on lost times . . .

Quantico, VA 1990

Joining the Navy had never been a question. He not only wanted to be a part of the same thing his father was, he relished in creating new records to outdo past generations. Getting past basic training seemed a breeze to him, where it had taken true push for others. He was made for this stuff. An all-star junior high and high school wrestler, track and swimmer, his whole life had prepared his body for this. He was a hard-core bad ass, and cocky to boot. His natural abilities and intelligence only enhanced his arrogance.

The only surprise was his desire to become a Navy medic. His superiors, family, and friends were thrown off guard because he had a general rough demeanor. There was a soft side to him, though, that not many ever saw. He wanted to use his God given abilities to help, not hurt.

It was his mother, who died when he was six years old, that motivated this decision. It was his duty to her which caused him to choose life, not death. That was until he found out the truth of why she died--then his duty became retribution for her sake . . .

Returning to the present, he finished counting out 1,000 crunches, and got into the shower for a brief cold one. Stepping out of the bathtub when finished, he briefly admired his powerfully built body in the full-length mirror at the end of the tub. As black as night, his skin seemed to leech all shade and shadow from the room. Running his finger along the length of the scar on his chest, he shuddered at how close he had come to death with that one. Yet even this only confirmed that he was doing the right thing. He was not a religious man any longer, but he did believe in Karma. Karma was the essence of his duty.

Still naked, he walked over to the kitchen counter and rolled out the long cloth which held the tools of his trade. Admiring all of the razor-sharp, metallically shiny, death dealing or life restoring instruments always aroused him.

Moving to the bed, The Surgeon lay down, and began stroking himself as he finalized his plans . . .

Chapter 1

Private Investigators Suck

Friday, May 12
12:06 a.m.

Mark St. James wrestled with his blankets in darkness. Finally snatching his cell phone off the night stand, he slurred a groggy "Hello." Pulling the phone from his ear and grimacing at the sound of the loud ringing, he pressed the send button and said, "Hello," again.

A female voice on the other end said, "We need you to come down to Izzolio's Family Restaurant. There's a situation we could use your assistance on."

Glancing at the clock he grumbled, "Christ almighty, Kidd, it's just after midnight. What's so important that you need me? I don't even work for you anymore, and you're busting my chops before six a.m.!"

Quincy Police Chief Heather Kidd replied, "Sorry, Mark, can't go into details, but do me a favor and get down here. Also, you might want to keep the early breakfast to a minimum. It's really nasty down here, and quite a few officers have already emptied their stomachs."

"Give me about an hour, and I'll be there," he mumbled.

He sat up in bed, rubbed his eyes, turned on the lamp, and stretched while yawning. Shuffling into the bathroom, he took what should have been his morning piss, and turned on the shower. Stripping out of his bed clothes, he got under the cold spray to fully wake up. After a few moments he adjusted the temperature to a more comfortable degree, then finished cleaning up.

Getting out of the shower, he looked at himself in the mirror and grimaced at the overgrown stubble on his face. He stood just over six feet, had a muscular build from his many days in the Navy, and could see the beginning of the slim line of hair which ran down his chest. His dark green eyes held an intense look most of the time these days, and his nose had a slight bend from the few times it'd been broken.

He was not a morning person. Since becoming a private investigator, after his resignation from the police department, he had grown fond of sleeping in till at least eleven. Being woken up in the middle of the night by the Chief hadn't occurred in close to three years. Whatever the reason he was needed, he knew he wouldn't like it.

After getting dressed, he walked through the hallway into the kitchen and started a pot of coffee. Caffeine was a must, especially working on two hours' sleep. Pulling out a box of wheat bran, he poured a bowl and ate while waiting on the coffee. Fuck, he couldn't even enjoy the morning paper!

He grabbed a thermos out of a cabinet, poured the coffee in, and snatched up his 9mm Glock. Heading out the back door, he got into his jet-black Mercedes Benz, started her up, then pulled out of the driveway and drove down Quincy Street. Taking a left on First, he took a sip of the hot coffee and reflected on the only reason the Chief would be calling on him.

He used to be the head of the Severe Crimes Investigation Unit at the Quincy Police Department. S.C.I.U. was pretty much his baby from top to bottom. Upon returning to the States while in the military, he'd found his hometown in the middle of major criminal degradation. Knowing at the time he couldn't do anything about it, he had made a decision to do so as soon as he could. So after completing his tour in the Navy, he did. He'd created Severe Crimes at the permission of the former Chief, and it still existed today under the new one.

Severe Crimes investigated all the major crimes, such as murder, robberies, sex cases, etc. The only difference between his unit and Robbery/Homicide was it handled all the habitual cases, a series of crimes by possibly the same offender. Earning a Master's in Criminal Psychology at Penn State had helped him develop an ability to understand the offender's psyche.

His main purpose in developing a unit for habitual offenders was to clean up the streets of the town he grew up in. He also wanted to do this to avenge his brother, who had been murdered when he was twelve years old. His brother's killer had never been caught. He went to college so he could help put away scum like that.

Growing up in Quincy, Pennsylvania, wasn't always easy. Even small towns had problems, especially the ones with colorful histories. Being kin to the founder hadn't made his life any easier. Then his younger brother had been killed. They had blamed it on a drifter, but he didn't know if he would ever know the truth. The unfortunate thing about death is most of the time the ones who die aren't heard. The majority of family and friends were supportive and sympathetic, but there are always the few assholes who just don't care. That's a story for another day, though.

A few months into S.C.I.U.'s first year, they had encountered the Unit's most serious case, and unfortunately Mark's last. A man named Melvin Flores had begun killing people. Melvin had been nicknamed The Hangman, due to how he killed his victims. He had been a formidable enemy. Shortly after the case was closed, Mark had taken a leave of absence, then eventually quit the department.

Pulling up behind the Medical Examiner's car, about half a block from Izzolio's, he was gonna have to walk the rest of the way. The street was unusually dark; even the street lamps were out. The only illumination came from all the car lights. Walking up to the restaurant, he stopped next to Kidd. Heather Kidd stood about half a foot shorter than he did at five eight. She wasn't a fat woman, yet a person wouldn't describe her as skinny either. He'd always thought she had a healthy set of love handles. Her chest had probably gotten many a man slapped for too much staring, and there was a great deal to grab in the back. She bore hazel blue eyes, full lips, and substantial dimples in her cheeks when she smiled. She had too many wrinkles under her eyes— though she was only 36, many years in a stressful job had written themselves in her face. Generally, she was a very kind, caring, and compassionate woman, though she was well known for her temper when angry. All things considered, she would most likely be a hell of a fuck. He wasn't interested in Kidd this way, though— besides, he'd heard her name fit her well, because she was a tease in bed. Looking down he asked, "Well, whatcha got?"

"It's really bad, multiple homicide. Couldn't talk on the phone due to the circumstances. Also, didn't think you'd believe me if I did anyway," saying the last with a little doubt herself. "I gotta warn you it's not a sight for the squeamish. It may be the worst you've seen."

Mark said, "That bad, huh? How many victims?"

"Twenty-eight was the last count."

"Holy shit, how in the world did someone manage that?"

"The details are still coming in, and we won't know the particulars till Hall is done, but did you notice the lack of electricity?"

"Yeah."

"A car took out a transformer pole a block down; the car was empty after the fire was put out. It appears the killer went to work under the cover of darkness. There's something else, and you're not gonna like it. After checking out the entire scene, the kitchen is why I called you."

"What happened in the kitchen?"

"You'll have to see it yourself, just don't break down on me. We think this is somehow connected to the Hangman."

"What! Why?"

"Just go check out the scene, Mark," she replied sympathetically.

Leaving Kidd outside, he walked through death's gate.

CHAPTER 2

DEATH BY NUMBERS

Friday, May 12
1:22 a.m.

The overpowering smell of iron, feces, and urine was still strong within the room. It told the tale of many deaths, not just one. Strangely, there was also a minor perfume smell, as if someone had tried to cover up the odor and given up when it did no good. It was like walking through a dead whore house. He heard the sound of a battery powered generator in the area.

There wasn't any lack of lights in this room. It seemed like going from a dark night to a bright afternoon. The police must have borrowed every lamp in the area to do this. The lamps certainly explained the sound of a generator. One thing for sure though: Kidd was right, this was not something anyone should ever have to see.

When he first walked in, all he could do was stop and wonder. Even being in the wars he'd been through hadn't prepared him for it. The senseless slaughter in Iraq during his first tour was almost pretty compared to this moment in time. Even he felt the little food in his stomach churn momentarily.

Looking around, he noticed a pale faced officer named Aaron standing guard at the door. He was an old timer, who probably was only there because he had already lost all of his stomach contents, and had learned to avoid looking at the scene. In fact, every time he saw it by happenstance he appeared to cringe. Mark had known Aaron while on the force and had gotten along with him. There was also a guard to his right at the kitchen door. Mark thought his name was Mike or David, something like that. He only knew him in passing, though. Walking about the room meticulously were Rebecca and her team.

Rebecca Hall was the Quincy Medical Examiner. She was the first of hopefully many M.E.'s in Quincy. She was eight years younger than Mark at 34, stood five four, and weighed about 110 soaking wet. She had raven black hair, soft cheek bones, a small nose, and a petite, but curvy upper lip, along with a strong succulent lower one. It was for this reason most people thought her smile brought the best out of everyone around her. The most unusual and stunning part of her was the color of her eyes: an astonishing violet. On many occasions, he'd lost track of his thoughts when looking into them. Her body was well proportioned in all the right places, and in truth he found her extremely attractive.

Rebecca and Mark knew each other very well. He had even babysat her when she was growing up. When she was ten, she had developed a crush on him, then he ended up going to college and joining the military. At first, she couldn't forgive him for what she saw as abandonment. Over time, and with maturity, she realized he hadn't done it to slight her.

Today he thought of his relationship with her as mutually close. They had never been romantic, but had come close on many occasions. He knew she cared deeply for him, but he just couldn't seem to get past the loss of his family. He was as close as he could be to a woman right now. She'd been his strength, and the reason he didn't drink anymore. If it weren't for her, he probably wouldn't be standing in this room. She'd stood by him ever since his wife and two children had been murdered three years ago.

Rebecca glanced at him, raised one finger to say they'd talk shortly, and continued with the scene. She appeared unaffected walking through a room filled with dead people, although he knew her better. He supposed being the M.E. for the Hangman had sort of cauterized her to situations like this one. She was good though. In fact, she wasn't only the first M.E. in Quincy, but was the best one in a hundred miles.

Stepping over to Aaron, he said, sympathetically, "Not the best night to be on duty."

Aaron replied weakly, "Wasn't my night, I was on call."

"It's a shame, wouldn't have wanted you to see this for the world. I tell you this job only seems to get worse."

"Got that right, I thought we'd got over deaths like this when you killed the Hangman. I mean what he did was god awful, but this," glancing at the carnage, and shuddering, "This is insanity, that's what it is." Then, with a hint of mercy, "Sorry to bring 'him' up, Mark."

"No problem—it seems I'll be dealing with it soon anyway, from what the Chief says."

"Yeah, sorry about that, too."

At that moment Jonathon Cole, his old partner, and current Homicide detective, walked through the kitchen door. Jonathon stood exactly six feet, and weighed 240. All of his weight was hard muscle. He worked out frequently at home and the Recreation Center. At 44 years of age, it was evident he had made sure the years were good to him. He had rusty brown hair, a large protruding nose, rather high cheek bones, and soft brown eyes. A lot of criminals, and ladies, had softened up staring into his eyes, for they appeared to be compassionate and caring. The mistake most people made was depending on his eyes. His friends knew him to be a fair man, but also a force to be reckoned with if crossed. Noticing him standing at the entrance, Jon walked over and stopped at his side.

"Thought the Chief might call you in on this one, Mark. Hope you are doing okay. This is bad, real bad. The worst I've seen. Even worse than you-know-who."

"You can say his name. It's been three years since I found Melvin Flores in my house and killed him. It's not like I'm still a little boy, Jon."

"Sorry, no need to be snippy!"

"Forgive me Jon, blame it on the lack of sleep. So, what do you know so far?"

"Well, first the M.E. believes the victims were still alive, somehow, when this was done. Second, he appears to be very skilled with a knife--it may have been a scalpel according to her. Since she's never wrong, I tend to believe her. And finally, he seems to be very knowledgeable of the body. Unfortunately, these deaths look like the work of a serial killer Interpol has called the Surgeon. He's an international killer, believed also to be a mercenary, but no one knows for sure."

"Where'd you hear about the Surgeon?"

"Well one of the junior detectives, who upchucked his entire supper last night and probably won't eat for a week, said the scene reminded him of a notice about the killer he happened to come across while researching the Hangman three years ago. You remember good ole Frank Soluchu, don't you? He was working research in the S.C.I.U., till you quit and they put Doug in control instead of me."

"Yeah, I remember. Good kid. Where's Stintz at anyway?"

"He's back in the kitchen. Couldn't stand my presence any more so he kicked me out."

"You wanna walk me through the scene, old partner?" Mark asked, still avoiding the next room. "Starting out here; that way you don't have to deal with the asshole again so soon."

"Sure," Jon replied, glancing knowingly at his ex-partner.

Walking to the southeast corner of the restaurant, Mark stood reluctantly outside of the scene, but close enough to see the bloodbath. The M.E. glanced at him briefly again, then continued directing the camera shots.

The most dominant part of the bizarre scene was the body laid out on the salad bar. He didn't know everyone in town, but unfortunately, he had known this woman. Ann Dietz used to be a nurse at the Quincy Medical Center. She was a very kind woman. She used to pay careful attention to his children when they had been there. Now she was dead, murdered in cold blood.

Splayed across the bar, she was completely nude. Her clothes had been neatly folded and lay on a table to the left of the bar. Her chest was laid open with a Y-incision. Her body, in a state of rigor mortis, looked almost petrified or frozen in shock. All of her internal organs had been removed, and each planted in its own bowl or container on the bar. Her stomach, liver, kidneys, spleen, bladder, lungs, heart, and intestines were each bathing in what appeared to be formaldehyde. The word malignant was drawn in blood on the window above the salad bar.

Forming a U around this were the rest of the victims. As if forced to be the audience to an autopsy, there were twenty-six men, women, and children sitting dead around Ann. Each member of the 'audience' had their throats neatly cut, and their tongue hanging from below their Adam's apple, cut in the form of a Colombian Necktie. He knew some of the victims. He wanted to howl at the loss of all these innocent lives.

What kind of monster could do this? Why would he? Even having a psychology degree hadn't prepared him for these questions. The names his mind conjures for the killer are useless, but probably accurate. He sheds a tear as he thinks about his own children. They too died in this manner. Robbed of the life they could have had.

Turning away he began to walk toward the kitchen door, but a delicate hand placed on his arm halted him. Turning toward Rebecca, she smiled a sad smile as she looks into his glistening eyes. As they stared into each other's eyes for a moment, everything that needed to be said was said.

In her strong, melodious voice she said, "I wanted to speak with you before you went into the next room. The Chief has probably already prepared you, but I wanted to personally send my love and be there when you see it. I took the liberty of getting her down to decrease the impact, but that is all. The pictures taken will suffice for the rest."

"What do you mean get her down, was she hanging like the others three years ago?"

"Yes, except we know this to be a copycat, because the body was mutilated horribly before being hung by her intestines. Very much unlike The Hangman's killings."

"Oh, so why does everyone believe there's a connection?"

"We don't think its coincidence. We think this was a direct message to you."

Glancing at the door, he nervously said, "Let's get this over with."

Walking with Rebecca to his left and Jon to his right, they move toward the kitchen and walk in the door. Feeling a hand squeeze his shoulder, he gasped in exhalation as memory floods through him.

Chapter 3

Anniversaries

Tuesday, June 17, 2003
9:05 p.m.

Today was his fifth anniversary and the job had him running ragged. This new case he was on was not only horrid, but time consuming. 'The Hangman' had already killed four families. Being the head detective and founder of Severe Crimes Investigation was exhausting, yet rewarding. He had been happy, up until now, cleaning up the streets.

Now he was working 'The Hangman' case. So far, the killer had made few mistakes. He believed he was getting close to his identity though. Although 'The Hangman' could be a woman, they at S.C.I.U. had ruled out the idea because of the kind of deaths and the strength it would take for the killer to pick up the bodies.

Driving down Second, he was finally on his way home to his wife, daughter, and son. He was supposed to be off shift at 4:30, but due to the seriousness of the case, shifts were indeterminable. He was looking forward to this night. His family was celebrating tonight. Molly and Brent did not fully understand the reason for the celebration, but he and Susan enjoyed their presence. He just hoped the meal wasn't cold. He had called and told her two hours ago he'd be home about 7:30.

His family gave him a relief from his job's grueling existence. He liked his job, but he loved his family. Molly would be five in a month and Brent just turned three two months ago. Molly was currently into Barbie, unicorns, and bright colors, whereas Brent just vied for attention. His favorite forms of gaining attention were coloring on walls and destroying his sister's dolls. The first was easy to fix with the new Crayola erasable markers. The second was trying, and frustrating, but he seemed to have been able to get Molly to understand it was just a phase. They were a handful, but he loved them more than any father could. Susan and he still had an almost child-like, innocent love for one another. It was more like adoration.

Rounding the corner of Oak Avenue, off of Main, he pulls into his driveway and parks. Grabbing his briefcase and stepping out of the car, he walked to the front door. Strolling into his living room the smell catches his attention immediately. Iron is heavy in the air. Wars had attuned him to the smell of death.

Abruptly he drops his briefcase and pulls his Glock out, all in one smooth motion. Sliding up against the nearest wall, he's already begun fearing the worse, but is preparing for anything as well. Starting with the front of the house he begins a systematic check, clearing each room as he went. The farther he goes in, the stronger the smell gets.

Pushing open his children's bedroom door, he cries out in rage and grief. Hanging from the ceiling by their own intestines, both of his children swing above their beds. His daughter's toes just barely brush the mattress, making a slight rustling noise. Their beds were covered in blood. A slight dripping from his son's toes tells him the deaths were recent, but obviously his body had been drained. Noticing this brought him to fear the worst, and motivates him on. If they were recent, then Susan could still be alive; it all depends on how long it takes for a three-year-old's blood supply to drain from the body. Not information anyone should have to know. Quickly doing an about face he takes the wall, and tries to walk stealthily to the next room. Knowing the yell already has given him away he knows he has to move fast.

Kicking the master bedroom door open, he sees his wife hanging above their bed, her ankles lying on the mattress, feet bent behind her. 'The Hangman' stands at the open window as if trying to leave. He hears himself *say, "Hey, asshole," and when The Hangman turns to face him, he sees fear on his face. Bringing up his arm up robotically, he shoots him between the eyes . . .*

Thursday, May 11, 2006
5:11 p.m.

Kiara sat in front of her vanity mirror doing final touches on her make up. Danny would be there to pick her up any moment. Today was their one-year anniversary, and he was taking her to Izzolio's to celebrate.

She was only eighteen years old, but she knew she was in love. She didn't know what would happen when she graduated next month because she planned on going to college. Several had accepted her, and all of them were two or three states away. She wanted to major in Art, but didn't know if she could handle the competition later.

Finishing her makeup, she noticed her hair slightly out of place and went to fixing it. Finally done she got up, straightened her dress, and headed toward her door. Hearing her mother call from the living room, "Kiara, Daniel's here," she smiled at her timing.

"Coming mom," she exclaimed.

Leaving her bedroom, she crossed the hall and entered into the living room. She smiled at Danny sitting on the loveseat. He wore a navy-blue button up with black khaki pants. Standing up he was the most handsome man she'd ever met. He had blue eyes, a medium sized nose, thin lips, high cheekbones, and a light olive skin tone. He was simply gorgeous.

Watching him look her up and down while licking his lips, she knew she was stunning. Dark brown curly hair framing her face, she had light green eyes, a petite nose, and full lips which had a slight pout to them. She wore an emerald-colored evening gown which highlighted her eyes and well-tanned skin. She then smiled as she watched his facial expression become shy, embarrassed, and almost lovesick.

Going to him and hugging, they sat back down on the love-seat for a few minutes of idle chatting with her parents before leaving. Looking at her mother, she asked, "So, how do we look together?" for probably the hundredth time.

"You both look as natural as any couple that's been together for years, honey. Congratulations on the anniversary. One year! I knew you two were meant for a long, happy relationship the first time I saw you together."

"I'm a bit surprised myself--what with the big scare I gave you in the beginning and all, son!" her father exclaimed.

"That's alright sir, I know what it's like being protective of the things I love. Not that your daughter is a 'thing,' sir!" Daniel said.

"Just remember what we discussed, son, especially about to-night, and you'll do just fine."

"Will do, sir."

"Is midnight okay, mom and dad, since it's a special occasion?"

"Yes honey, go and enjoy yourself," they said in unison, and then shared a knowing look among themselves.

Getting up, they headed to the door, Danny grabbed his black sports jacket and they went outside. Heading to the car she asked, "So, you mind telling me what my dad and you discussed, as well as the look that passed between them before we left?"

"It was nothing, sweetheart. They were just telling me about their first anniversary, and your dad made some gentlemanly sug-gestions."

"Oh, well, I think you're the most-gentle man I've ever met. I love you, Danny," she murmured, then squeezed his hand.

Holding the door open for her, she got into the passenger's seat, then he closed it. Going around the front, Danny got into the driver's seat of his 1996 Buick. It was an old car, but he liked it and it was his first. Pulling out onto States Avenue, he went up the road and took a right on Main.

As Kiara took Danny's right hand, they were comfortable in the silence. Glancing at one another occasionally they admired each other's bodies and smiled. Finally, he asked, "What do you think our lives will be like when we graduate?"

Considering how much his question reflected on her earlier thoughts, she answered, "I'm not sure, you know I want to go to Art School, and I'd like to stay with you. I love you Danny, but I don't want to hold you back or drag you after me and have you regret it later."

"I love you too, Ki, and I'd never regret being with you. Wherever you go, if I come, I'm sure I can get a job or even go to college online. We'll discuss it more tonight, we're here baby," he replied pulling into the restaurant's parking lot.

Getting out the car, he strolled around the front and opened the door for her. They embraced and kissed briefly before heading toward the restaurant. Entering Izzolio's, she admired the restaurant's interior decorating. Everything was done in black and white decor. There were about twenty tables with white linen tablecloths, and high-backed black cushioned chairs. Each table had two to six chairs, one or two lit candles, and the unoccupied ones had a black rolled up napkin which held the silverware. A basket of fresh, buttered Italian bread was at every table.

There were two waiters and three waitresses attending the customers, while the maitre d' stood waiting to welcome new customers. Approaching Enzio, the maitre d', Danny told him their names, and that they had a reservation, then waited.

"Yes, I see you here on our list. Would you like a window seat or something more private," glancing briefly, yet conspiratorially, at Danny. "Window is fine . . . private will do," both of us spoke simultaneously. Glancing at one another for a moment, Danny looked at Enzio and stated, "Window seats, I'm sure the Quincy Medical Center's lawn is beautiful this time of night."

Going to their seats, Danny and Kiara sat down and began looking through the menus Enzio gave them, occasionally looking up at each other and giggling. Mikaela, their waitress, approached and asked if they were ready to order. Danny told her no, but that he wanted a Coke for himself and a Pepsi for Kiara. The waitress said "OK" and went to get the drinks.

Looking into Kiara's eyes, Danny said dramatically, "I want this evening to be special. I know it's the most expensive in town, but please have whatever you want. This night is about us, and I've been saving up for it for two months."

As she was about to respond, the waitress returned to place the drinks on the table, along with a vase with half a dozen pink roses in it. At Kiara's wondering glance, Mikaela told her the roses were ordered when the reservations had been made last month.

Looking lovingly at Danny, she said, "They're beautiful; you're certainly off to a good start."

He smiled in embarrassment, and, looking at the waitress told her, "I'll have the Parmesan with Pork Sausage, Spinach, and Double Fudge Cake for dessert," then looked inquiringly across the table at Kiara.

"I'll have Stuffed Shells with Shrimp Sauce, Broccoli in smothered cheese, and please send a large slice of his dessert. We'll share it."

Taking their order, Mikaela nodded then headed back toward the kitchen.

While waiting on their food, the two talked leisurely about school, Danny's construction job, and their families. Socializing with Danny was so easy. Most people thought him to be dumb because he didn't have many friends and choose construction as an occupation. Danny was actually very intelligent, and knew how to hold a conversation. This is one of the things which drew her to him.

She was shocked at how much they had in common when they first started dating. Now it seemed second hand for them to finish each other's sentences. Munching on some of the warm Italian bread, she reflected on how they must replace it frequently. The bread made her mouth water from the intense garlic butter flavor.

Coming back to the table, Mikaela interrupted the couple briefly to bring their food, then left them to themselves. Eating slowly, they enjoyed their meal and even laughed as we tried feeding one another occasionally. At one point Danny wiped Kiara's mouth with his finger because she had dribbled shrimp sauce down her chin. Before they knew it, it was about eight and dessert had arrived.

As they begin to settle down to enjoy their dessert, he took her hand, looked into her eyes, and said, "We've been together a year today, Ki, and you know I love you. I've been thinking about us all month long. I want to be with you wherever you go in life." As he paused, she watched him swallow, pull a case from his pocket, then come around the table and kneel down in front of her. Trembling in shock, admiration, love and fear she listened as he said, "I love you with all my heart, Kiara. I want to spend the rest of my life with you. Will you marry me?"

Still trembling slightly in shock, she mumbled, "Can you excuse me for a moment?"

Walking unsteadily to the restroom, she stumbled into a stall and vomits her supper into the toilet. Picking herself up, she moved to the window, pushed it up and swallowed long breaths of fresh night air. Going to the sink, turning on the cold water she splashed it on her face and rinsed her mouth out. This engagement came as a complete surprise. Of course, they'd talked about their future over the last month, but he never even hinted at this. She knew she loved him, but she was only eighteen, and he nineteen. Was this really the best thing for them?

Gathering herself up and collecting her thoughts seemed to take forever. She couldn't make him wait much longer. Rinsing her face and swishing water through her mouth again, she popped a mint, then left the restroom just as the lights went out.

There were several screams, then complete silence. Stopping outside of the restroom, she could barely see in the darkness. Waiting for her eyes to adjust, it suddenly dawned on her that she couldn't hear anything. No one was moving, and she couldn't even hear anyone talking. The employees should have been at least reassuring people.

It was then that she saw the shadow. Immediately she saw the shadow form teeth as its face sneered and it began to come toward her. She turned at once and ran into the pitch-black restroom. Moving to the window she began climbing out, and then fell to the pavement scraping her hands and knees. Getting up, she realized she had lost a shoe. As she began to run down the alley, she looked back and sees a smiling face in the moonlight, looking out the window.

CHAPTER 4

WHAT HAPPENS IN DEATH

Friday, May 12
1:12 p.m.

Mark arrived at the Quincy Medical Examiner's Office, which resided in the northeast corner of the Quincy Medical Center's basement, shortly after one in the afternoon. After leaving the scene this morning, he had gone home hoping that he'd fall asleep from mere exhaustion, but his mind kept conjuring up photos from his memory of three years ago. Memory was funny that way. When you needed to remember something, your mind firmly shut the door. Then when you least needed, or wanted, to use your memory, it gave you full access. He thought God was a very cruel man sometimes.

Walking into Rebecca's office, he found his plan to miss the traffic hadn't worked out. In front of Rebecca's desk, both chairs were in use. In the first sat the new S.C.I.U. head investigator, Detective Douglas Stintz. Stintz was an ambitious investigator. At 32, he was the youngest and smartest Special Detective in Quincy. Mark disliked his hard, arrogant personality, but had to admit that he was good at his job. He had an attractive, boyish looking face which seemed to compel people to open up. Short cropped black hair, brown eyes, a slight bridged nose, and thin lips made him almost too handsome. It was no wonder that women seemed to swoon over him. Stintz was not a humble man. The attention, and the fact that he knew that he was good at what he did, made him prideful and full of arrogance. Sitting up straight, he seemed to be preening himself--every few minutes he smoothed his hair down, as if a hair had somehow come loose since his last check. In the other chair sat Jon, the Homicide Detective assigned to the case. Apparently, Mark had arrived just in time to hear the beginning of a turf war.

"I don't give a fuck if this is considered a 'severe crime' or not, it is still a multiple homicide, which gives me the right to be here," Jon said heatedly.

"And all I'm telling you is to not step on my toes. Kidd made my unit the head of this investigation. Therefore, I will lead all questioning, and take point on everything else," Stintz spoke arrogantly.

"Um, hmm," clearing his throat, "I'm not interrupting anything am I?" he said, looking at Rebecca and winking.

The two reactions from the men couldn't have been more different. Jon just looked up and smiled, but Doug gave him a glare that would have killed, if he'd had laser vision. It was obvious Mark was just another obstruction to his case.

"Well, now that everyone that Kidd told me is supposed to be here, is, maybe we can get back to what really matters. Frankly, I don't care how you conduct yourselves outside of my office, however, while you're here, you guys will be professional. You see, I have a lot of respect for the dead. The victims of this crime were people. I will kick anyone out of my office who does not conduct themselves appropriately." Looking at Jon and glaring, "And you should know better. Does anyone have a problem with this?"

"No ma'am," Jon said.

"No," Doug responded gruffly.

Knowing Mark wouldn't be a problem, Rebecca didn't expect an answer from him.

"Good. Now, first of all, due to how recently these killings happened and the overwhelming number of bodies, I was able to get only four autopsies done since this morning. I didn't want to do more because of how tired I am. I have delegated most of the remaining bodies to my assistants, but I will be completing several more myself, over the next couple of days. I will also do a thorough follow up on what my assistants do. The bodies I chose to do myself were the main victim laid out on the salad bar, two from the victims in the dining room, and the victim from the kitchen.

Let's begin with the victim from the bar, whom we will refer to as Ann from now on. Ann was more or less disemboweled in much the same way as an autopsy is done. The major difference, I want to note, is that apparently from the massive blood loss, Ann was still alive when it was done. I do not know if she was conscious during the murderer's actions, but she was alive. And before you ask, I have yet to determine how this was possible. After doing an extensive search of her hands and body, there were no visible defense marks, so I can rule out that she fought back. However, with a crime this brutal, I will rule out that she cooperated. I've done blood work on all the victims and I'd bet my life that drugs were involved.

Now, as I said, Ann was brutally murdered by a sadistic and smart killer. Every move he or she made was as precise as I'd ask of any of my assistants. Most likely, the killer is male because of the strength it took to carry some of the victims. The Y-incision was precise. I believe the weapon was a set of surgeons' blades. The only vital organ not removed was the brain. All of Ann's internal organs were removed and placed in a substance similar to formaldehyde, though it wasn't formaldehyde. We won't know what it was 'till the tox screen returns. The final notable thing about Ann was that her tongue was removed and wasn't recovered from the scene of the crime. I believe the killer took it. Any questions so far?"

No one spoke.

"Alright then, the next two victims, designated 'A' and 'B', because of the lack of identification found on them, were killed in the exact same manner. First, their throats were cut from the right to the left, which would make our killer either left-handed or ambidextrous. My vote, by partial examination of the other victims, is left-handed, because all of the victims' knife point origins were on the right. Once again, the victims were alive as evidenced by the massive loss of blood. Both arteries on the neck were cut cleanly. The blood splatter alone from the arteries squirting is evidence of a rapid heartbeat. Again, both 'A' and 'B' showed no signs of defense against their attacker, but there is a clear sign that both were in distress by the blood splatter. The final note is, instead of taking the tongues, both victims' tongues were hanging from their throats. Again, we see evidence of a killer with prior medical knowledge. The frenum was cut, and the killer meticulously pulled the tongue through the slit in the esophagus and out of the neck. I believe that the victims were dead at this point, due to the lack of blood on the tongue itself. Besides the lack of blood in the body, the rest of the autopsy was standard, with no unusual findings. I did not find any foreign matter on the bodies to provide to the lab. Which, by the way, was true of Ann as well. Another clue which tells me our killer is smart. Again, are there any questions before I move to the final autopsy victim?"

This time Mark spoke up and asked "You spoke of blood splatter. I'm assuming that the killer had to walk through all of the blood. Was there any evidence around the victims to suggest this?"

"None that I saw, Mark, although there were some unusual pattern marks in the blood on the ground. You would have to talk with the forensic team to find out what those were," she responded.

"How similar were the cuts in length to each other on the victims?" Stintz asked.

"Fairly close, they were all about 9 inches in length across the throat. They differed by no more than half an inch. Why?"

"I just thought we could determine how long the killer's arms might be, which would help approximate a height."

"Good thought there. I'll have my assistants get an exact measurement later and send it to your e-mail. Any other questions? Okay, good. My final autopsy was a very brutal murder." Rebecca continued, "The victim was the restaurant's owner. Amanda's murder was different from the others. Once again, as evidenced by the bruising and blood loss the victim was alive. However, what was done to her appears to be out of rage. Amanda had multiple contusions on her face, breasts and mid-section. The femur bones in both of her legs were fractured. And her entire body was cut with a razor blade 112 times in areas which would bleed, but not cause death.

The cause of death was what is known as a Hangman's Fracture. The killer sliced Amanda's stomach open and then used her intestines to hang her from the kitchen ceiling rack. After letting the victim go, her weight and the drop caused a fracture of her upper cervical vertebrae. I believe the killer purposely fractured both femur bones so Amanda couldn't stop herself from being hung.

Due to the brutality of the crime, I tend to think that we have two killers. However, since the victim appeared to have been paralyzed, like the other victims, and the blade used to cut Amanda seems like the same one as the one used on the other victims, I can't be sure. What I am sure of, is that something about Amanda annoyed the killer or killers. It's also a distinct possibility that this was personal," glancing at Mark but leaving the verbalization of this threat to him unspoken, "Are there any questions? No? Good. Now for what could be some good news."

"There is actually some good news in the middle of all of this horror?" Jon interjected.

"Yes, it appears that there may be someone unaccounted for at the scene."

"What makes you think that?" Stintz asked.

"Because, when going through the victim's personal effects, I found a discrepancy, which led me to call Detective Luis at Q.P.D.

to inquire about the reservation book confiscated from the scene. I found an engagement ring. The discrepancy was that there appeared to be no one there for the victim to give it to."

Both Jon and Stintz leaned forward with anticipation as Rebecca continued.

"According to the reservation book a party of two was listed as arriving together. One Daniel Verin and one Kiara Benson. After finding this out I got on the net to review the crime scene photos. There is one person missing. I believe Kiara somehow got away!"

"That is good news. A very promising lead you've discovered, Ms. Hall," Stintz proclaimed.

"You can talk to Luis about contacting Daniel's parents. I checked, and the Benson's aren't listed in the phone book."

"Very well, I'll take it from here. Thank you for your help and medical expertise," Stintz said.

Getting up to leave, Jon looked at Stintz and said, "Don't forget to keep me informed on this lead. I want to be there when you question the witness."

"Fine," Stintz responded abruptly. Stintz then pulled out a cell and began dialing as he got up to leave.

After Jon and Stintz left, Rebecca looked at Mark and asked, "How are you doing?"

Staring into her fierce violet eyes, he responded, "I'll survive."

"Want some company tonight?"

Moving to leave, he replied, "No, some demons just never go away. I'll see you later."

Walking out of her office and down the hall he could feel her eyes following him until he turned the corner.

CHAPTER 5

FIRST LEADS

Friday, May 12
4:02 p.m.

Arriving at the Verin residence, Mark waited for Jon and Stintz to show up before approaching, because he wasn't any longer a part of the Q.P.D. Chief Kidd had assigned him as a consultant on the case due to his education and history. Already the case had him baffled. How were the victims paralyzed? Why was there only one hanged victim? Was it a direct message to him? Did the killer know him personally? He was obviously a very meticulous and smart killer. He seems to know a lot about medical practices. Was he a doctor?

So many unanswered questions. Glancing at his watch, he began tapping his foot in impatience. He was hoping that they would arrive soon. With a case this big, all leads had to be followed up on. The possible witness, who was unaccounted for at the restaurant, was a major lead.

Watching the two cars pull up, he got out of his vehicle as Jon and Stintz exited theirs. Mark watched as Jon stepped back to let

Stintz approach the door first, since he technically had charge of the case.

Mark did not like to be around Stintz. He was an asshole, plain and simple. While Jon should have gotten to be the lead investigator for the S.C.I.U., since he had been the number two man under Mark, Kidd had given Stintz the job. He knew this had upset Jon, but she had chosen the most qualified man to replace him, whether he liked it or not.

Knocking on the front door while Jon and Mark hung back, Stintz looked very dignified in his blue pin striped suit. A woman who appeared to be in her early forties answered the door. She wore her raven black hair pulled back in a bun, and had hazel eyes, a friendly smile, and slight crow's feet at the corners of her eyes. Not an obese woman by any means, she was plump and looked well fed. Wearing a white, loose cotton dress with butterflies above its hem, she was a beautiful woman, despite the anxious look on her face.

"Are you Mrs. Verin, ma'am?" Stintz asked.

"Yes, but you can call me Shirley, and who are you?"

"Detective Doug Stintz of the Q.P.D., S.C.I division."

"Are you following up on my phone call to the report that my son didn't return home last night?"

"In a way, yes. Can my associates and I come in please, ma'am?" Stintz responded reservedly.

"Sure, just take your shoes off at the door." Walking into the hallway atrium, Mark admired the Verin households' home. Beside the front door was a wall-mounted coat rack with shoes neatly lined up underneath, along the wall. Through the left entryway was the dining room and the kitchen, and through the right was the living room. Hanging on all of the walls, leading to the back of the house, were what Mark assumed to be family photos and memorabilia.

Mark slipped his shoes off, and his colleagues did the same at the request of Mrs. Verin. He set them nicely beside the others. Following Stintz and Jon, he walked into the living room and leaned against one of the walls.

The living room was cozy, with everything centered nicely. In the middle sat a medium-sized oak end table, rectangular in shape. It had an assortment of magazines, remote controls, and drinks sitting on it. The drinks were on coasters, of course. Surrounding the coffee table was a couch and two armchairs. Directly in front of the couch was a beautiful 48-inch Samsung television, with a Samsung 5.1 home theater system connected. The rest of the room was decorated with photos and knickknacks which conjured up a homey warmness.

As Shirley took a seat on the couch, a little girl of about seven or eight, walked in and asked, "Mommy, what's going on?"

Shirley responded, "Nothing Rachelle, mommy just needs some time alone with these gentlemen. I'll come and talk with you later, dear. Go finish your homework for now."

"But all I have left is math. You know I need help with that."

"I know darling, but I really need to talk with these men right now. Go out and play for now, and we'll work on math later."

Brightening up a bit, as if play time before homework was a treat, Rachelle smiled and laughed, then said, "Okay, Mommy, love you," as she turned and ran toward the back of the house.

Looking at Stintz, who had taken a seat in one of the armchairs, she said, "Sorry about that, my youngest can be a handful at times. Now, what is it you needed? Is my son in trouble? Did you find him?"

"That's no problem, ma'am. We're here because we need to ask you some questions about your son, Daniel."

"Why, is he okay? What's going on?"

"If you will just take a few deep breaths and wait until I've asked my questions, we can discuss your son further."

Shirley's voice was raising slightly in panic. She asked, "What's going on? Do I need to call an attorney? Is this serious? I don't understand!"

"No ma'am, it's nothing like that. I just need you to calm down, because we need you clear headed when you answer the questions," Stintz replied with a hint of impatience.

Noticing Jon glance at him as if to say this isn't starting well, Mark moved away from the wall and said, "Shirley, is it?" She nods, "My name is Mark St. James. As Detective Stintz informed you earlier, I'm an associate of the Q.P.D. I apologize for the confusion my colleague has caused. You do not need a lawyer. Your son hasn't done anything wrong. The detective is correct about remaining calm, though. May I be frank with you?"

Shirley visibly calmed down somewhat and replied, "Please, do!"

"Was your son at Izzolio's last night, and possibly with someone?"

"Yes, he was supposed to take Kiara, his girlfriend there last night."

"I'm sorry to be the one to tell you this, but your son died there last night."

"What! No, that's not possible. I called there last night after he didn't come home. The person that answered the phone said that everything was alright, and that he personally saw Daniel leave with Kiara."

Looking at Jon and Stintz with confusion, he looked back at her and asked, "What time did you call the restaurant?"

"Shortly after eleven. Why?"

Realizing this could be a very good lead, all three spoke at the same time. "Did the man identify himself?"... "What did he sound like?"..."Did you recognize the voice?"...

Looking at all them in confusion, Shirley didn't respond at all to the barrage of questions.

"Sorry about that. What we mean to say is, did you recognize the voice of the man you spoke with or did he identify himself?"

"Um mm . . . no I didn't and he didn't. Why?"

Looking momentarily at Stintz, who grudgingly nodded, Mark replied, "Shirley, I truly am sorry for your loss. You can identify the remains at the hospital when we're done here. Jon will even drive you if necessary. The information you are about to hear has not been made public, yet. Last night there was a multiple homicide at Izzolio's, and your son was one of the many victims.

The Medical Examiner found an engagement ring in the pocket of your son's clothes, and table assignments listed in the restaurant's registration book led us to believe that there was someone unaccounted for. It was this person that brought us here today."

She was visibly in shock and starring blank eyed at him. Squatting down, he carefully took one of Shirley's hands and looked into her vacant eyes. After a few moments, he cleared his throat, and said, "I'm very sorry, but we think the man you spoke with last night may have been the killer. That is why we need you to bear with us for a few more minutes. Can you do that?" Tears began to run down Shirley's face as she started blinking to clear her vision and nodding, she choked out, "Yes. Oh, God, my poor Daniel!"

Giving her a few minutes more to calm down somewhat, he just remained squatting beside her and held her hand. All of this was bringing way too many memories of being in the Q.P.D. back to him. Without even knowing it, this woman was giving him strength as well.

Finally, he asked, "Can you remember any details about this phone conversation you had?"

Taking a deep breath, she responded, "No, not really. He never gave a name or even identified the restaurant like they normally do, but I just thought they were busy. I was a little distracted though, because of Daniel being late.

When the man responded, he was very polite, so it just never clicked in my mind that he didn't identify the restaurant."

"Are you sure? Anything at all may help. Background noises, his voice tone, an accent, any of those type of things."

"Well, now that you mention it, it was quiet in the background. Oh, God, I should have known something was wrong then. Oh, what have I done? I should have known!"

Squeezing her hand and patting her leg comfortingly, he told her, "No, you've done nothing wrong. It isn't your fault. These things aren't something you're trained to recognize. Even someone who wasn't worried about a loved one most likely wouldn't have noticed."

Looking into his eyes, as if he were a rock to cling to in her newly broken world, she nodded. Taking a few deep breaths, she said, "The only thing I can remember, besides what I've already told you, is that he had a southern accent. Not the ya'll type, but more of a drawl to his words. It sounded like a southern type, but more refined. Like he was educated, maybe."

"That's good enough. You've done very well. Even this will help us find your son's killer. One final question. Have you heard from your son's girlfriend?"

"No. Oh, please, find her Mr. St. James. Please, make sure she's okay."

"Thank you, Shirley. I will do everything I can. When you're ready, you can identify your son's body at the Quincy Medical Center. Just ask for Rebecca Hall. Is there anything else we can do? Is there anyone we can call?"

"No, my husband's at work. I'll call him in a little bit."

"Okay, if you need anything or can think of anything else, just call the Q.P.D. and ask for Jon or you can call me at my number on this card." Mark then laid his business card on the coffee table.

4:40 p.m.

Walking to his car, he had begun pulling out his cell to call Kidd when Stintz grabbed his arm. Looking at him, he heard Stintz say, "Look, I appreciate the help in there, but this is still my investigation. Don't think you can just stroll in as an advisor and take things over. You understand me?"

"Yeah, sure, it's your ball. Take my advice though, you may want to learn to be a little more tactful in the future."

"How I do my job is none of your fucking business, Mr. Sensitivity!"

"Listen, asshole, I know we don't get along and I know that this is your case, so if you want me to back off, I will. Jon can keep me apprised of the situation. Now, take your hand off of me before you lose it!"

Releasing him, Stintz replied, "Fine, just so we're straight on who's running the show."

Watching him walk back to his car, Jon and Mark stood in silence. Jon just knew it wasn't time for talking—Mark just needed a breather after that encounter. After Stintz drove away, Mark called Kidd.

"Hey, it's me. Listen, I need you to get a cruiser over to 302 South States Avenue. Our possible witness lives there."

"What's the name, Mark?"

"Kiara Benson. She was the victim's girlfriend. The mother claims she went to the restaurant with him last night."

"Okay. I'll send one right away."

"Has the media been handled yet?"

"Yeah, it's supposed to be on the five o'clock news."

"Great, won't have to wait long on the panic."

"Look, Mark, you know we couldn't keep them away from a story like this. Most of the details are fuzzy for them. Hopefully it won't be as bad as you say."

"Yeah, that's the same thing your predecessor said too."

"Always the pessimist."

"That's right. Bye, Kidd."

"Talk to ya later."

Folding the cell shut, he said to Jon, "Well, let's go find out how badly Stintz fucks up the next interview."

Chapter 6

Kiara

Friday, May 12
1:09 p.m.

She was running in a grassy meadow. She knew not from what, only that her fear of something forced her on. When she looked back, all she saw were shadows, but they scared her. Everything was a blur when she looked left or right.

She could feel the damp grass under her bare feet and, for the first time she looked down. Startled by the sight of her sweat soaked, naked body, she stumbled. Why was she naked? Where were her clothes? What was she running from?

Looking back again, she saw a more solid, shadowy form move ahead of the others. Yelling, she tried to run faster and stubbed her toe on a rock. She could feel herself falling forward in pain and then she saw a bright light.

Suddenly, she was sitting in front of Daniel at the restaurant. Across from her, he was eating while mumbling things that she couldn't understand. All of a sudden, the meal was over and he was pulling something out of his pocket. An unnatural fear took hold of her and she got up and ran away.

When she looked back, his words no longer sounded garbled and she understood them clearly. He kept repeating, "Why did you leave me here? You abandoned me. I'm all alone." Then she saw a shadowy figure rise up behind him with a shiny object in his hand and the lights went out.

Struggling under the sheets, holding her down, she could hear someone screaming. Realizing it was herself, she stopped and surveyed her surroundings. She was in a hospital bed, the walls were an institutional, sky-blue color, and monitors were beeping at her bedside. The sheets were soaked with her sweat and she felt sticky from the dirt and sweat on her skin.

A nurse was at her side, as if materializing out of the air. "Are you okay, honey? You were screaming in your sleep. Oh, my, you're soaked. Let's get your bedding changed."

"Huh? What's going on? How did I get here?"

"No one's told you yet? Well, let me see if I can find a doctor."

Leaving the room as quietly and smoothly as she had apparently entered, she returned a little bit later with another woman behind her.

"Hi, my name is Dr. Moore. I wasn't here when you arrived last night, so I wasn't the first to treat you. What's your name? Do you remember that much?"

"Um, I'm Kiara. Kiara Benson. What happened to me? Where're my parents? How did I get here?"

With a look of sympathy, the doctor went on to say, "You were in a car accident. From the report I read briefly this morning while you were out, it appears you ran out in front of a car at the corner of Second and Main. Do you remember anything from last night?"

"All I remember is going to a restaurant with my boyfriend, Daniel, then I woke up here. Does my family know that I'm here?"

"Honey, we didn't know your name 'til just now. As soon as we get your contact information, we can notify your family. I'm sure they are very worried about you. Also, you should know the man, whose car you ran in front of, has been here all night. He brought you to the Emergency Room. Would you like to see him? Otherwise, we can tell him you're okay."

"I'm still feeling dizzy and kind of out of it. My legs hurt, too. I think I'll wait on visitors. But, can you call my mom and dad?"

"What's their phone number?"

"(412) 555-0697"

"I'll go do that right now. The nurse can see to your bed changing and some pain medication. Just rest easy for now. You're in safe hands."

The doctor and nurse left her to her own thoughts. What happened last night? Why couldn't I remember? Where was Daniel? Why wasn't he here? Everything was fuzzy to her. It was like waking up in a world where everything was weighted down by molasses.

The nurse returned and introduced herself as Sara, then gave her a Lortab for the pain. Helping her out of the bed, she escorted her to the bathroom. Untying the hospital gown for her, she says, "That must have been a nasty dream, honey. I haven't seen so much sweat on a body since my youngest watched his first horror movie. My husband is still paying for that choice."

Nodding her head instead of trying to explain the nightmare that still had her trembling inside, she stepped into the shower stall. Allowing the nurse to remove her gown and adjust the shower water, she returned to trying to puzzle her way through the haziness of her memory. She could hear the nurse making idle chit chat in an effort to be comforting, but alone in her thoughts the words were muted.

Finishing the uncomfortable shower, she stepped out and allowed Sara to carefully pat her body dry, so she wouldn't cause any of her many cuts to bleed again. Taking her back to bed Sara draped the fresh gown over her body so she could redress her wounds. Obviously, another attendee had changed the linen while she was in the shower because the sheets were crisp and dry.

Still trying to put the pieces of the last twelve hours of her life together she realized Sara was staring at her as if waiting for a response to a question. "I'm sorry, what was that?"

"That's alright sweetie. I asked, how are you feeling other than leg pain," she repeated.

"I guess okay. My back hurts a little, I'm dizzy occasionally, and my vision blurs frequently."

"The pain medication will help your back too, but I'll report the vision and dizziness because it could indicate you have a concussion. Now, is there anything I can get you when I'm done patching you up, a sedative perhaps?"

"No! I don't want to sleep right now," she blurts out, then, "I'm sorry, the nightmare is fresh that's all, but I am hungry."

"That's okay dear. I'll have them bring you something to eat. There ya go, all patched up. Let me see to the food and make a report on those things you mentioned."

Lying back in bed, she allowed Sara to replace the chest nodes for the heart monitor, and the rest of the gadgets which constantly kept track of her body functions. When she was done, Sara tucked the bed coverings around her, and asked, "How's that? Are you comfortable?"

"Yes. That's fine, thank you," Kiara replied.

"If you need anything, just push that button there," she pointed to a button on her bedside rails, "and if you want to watch TV here is the remote. Someone should be by shortly with something to eat. I'm sure the doctor will be by as well, to let you know about your family and check on you."

"Thank you, Sara."

Watching Sara leave, a slight pang of regret and fear rose within her. She did not know why, but she was afraid to be alone. It was an unnatural fear and reminded her of when she was a child. Her body trembled for a moment, and then stilled when she forced herself to take some deep breaths.

Turning the TV on, she randomly flipped through the channels. Finding an animated movie playing on one of the channels, she stuck with it. About a half hour later an attendee brought in some watered down, unsalted chicken soup, Jell-O, yogurt, and warm cider for her to eat. By the time she finished the meal the movie was over and the doctor had come back.

Dr. Moore said, "Well I contacted your family. Your dad was at work, so your mom is going to pick him up and then come here. They should be here soon. About your vision and dizziness, two or three times over the next twenty four hours, I'm gonna have the nurse do a check up on you. If your vision doesn't get better and the dizziness doesn't go away, we'll have to keep you longer. Otherwise, you should be able to return home tomorrow sometime. Okay?"

"Okay."

"Now I've briefly talked to your mom about your situation, but when they get here, I'll provide them with more information. Any improvement to your memory?"

"Thank you, and no."

"Well, you just rest and watch TV. If you need help sleeping later, we can give you a sedative."

"Thanks, but I'll be fine."

"Talk to you later, Kiara."

Settling down, she continued watching TV while she waited on her parents.

CHAPTER 7

REFLECTIONS

Friday, May 12
6:02 p.m.

Driving up First, Mark was almost glad not to have gotten a repeat of the interview. He had no idea where the Bensons were, and was worried about the witness Kiara. Upon arriving at the Benson residence about forty-five minutes ago, he'd found the cruiser he had called Kidd about, already there. He'd also seen Stintz ringing the door bell, apparently with no response. The evidence of impatience was written all over his body language.

Stintz finally walked back to the cruiser, spoke briefly with the two men inside, got into his car and drove away. Knowing both of the cops in the cruiser from the days on the force, he got out of his Benz and walked over. Gary Heid and Tom Jenson weren't rookies anymore. Both were good cops, though still a mite wet behind the ears.

Approaching the cruiser, he said, "Hey, Gary, Tom. Now, I'm assuming Stintz told you not to talk to me about the case, since it's his case and all—but even you guys know he's full of himself."

"Yeah, yeah. Look, Mark, you know we wouldn't deny you anything anyway," Gary replied. "Besides, Stintz doesn't overrule Kidd, and we're under orders from the Chief to keep you in the loop."

"Thanks, that makes my life easier. Let me know if anyone shows up, okay?"

"Sure thing."

"Also, in case you didn't know, I had my number changed again recently because of prank calls. Kidd has it if you need it."

"No problem, Mark. See you later."

Pulling onto Quincy Street, he approached his house, drove into the driveway, and turned off the engine. He had been driving aimlessly, mulling over the day's findings, when he had almost gotten into a car accident. Realizing he needed sleep, he drove home. Getting out of the car, he walked into the kitchen. He chose to hang onto his Glock due to the developing situation.

Heading into the bathroom, he stripped and got under a hot spray of water. Feeling his muscles loosen, he sighed in pleasure as his body relaxed. Closing his eyes, he felt his mind wander. His heart began to ache as memories of his family returned.

Susan had never been a shy woman. While I was on leave, she walked up to me at a bar to ask for a drink. As soon as I saw her my heart almost stopped. She smiled when I said, "Ah, sure." Her face in that moment was a slice of heaven.

Susan looked beautiful in her wedding gown. Her hazel eyes sparkled beneath the veil as she said, "I do." Lifting the veil, I warmly kissed my new wife on her full, pouting lips. Parting, we whispered, "I love you forever," to each other.

Looking down at my newborn baby daughter's beautiful face, I smile with pride. Glancing at Susan, I say, "Damn, that's one beautiful girl. She's gonna break someone's heart someday." As if on cue, my daughter laughed for the first time.

Walking down the hallway with Molly holding my hand, we stop before the classroom door. Molly glances up at me, clearly frightened by this new experience. I tell her, "Don't worry about it. You'll do fine. You're already the best in class to me, honey." She smiles, then walks through the door. I see all the kids look at her and several approach her to introduce themselves. Turning away, I smile.

Coming home from the hospital, I find Molly at home playing with Tia, the babysitter. As soon as Molly looks up and sees Susan and her newborn brother Brent, she yells in joy. Running toward Susan, she screams, "Mommy, Mommy, can I hold him?" Tears fill my eyes as I enjoy my daughter's enthusiasm.

Pushing Molly on the swing while keeping an eye on Brent in the stroller, I listen as my daughter tells me all the sordid details of her day in school. Smiling to myself, I think about how wonderful my two kids are.

Squealing with joy as Brent hugs his new Tickle Me Elmo toy, I can hear Molly in her first Barbie Dream Car as I take snapshots of my son's first Christmas. Looking at my wife, I wink.

Pulling his mind back to the present, he found that he had started crying. Wiping the tears from his eyes and rinsing his face off, he got out of the shower and dried off. Sliding into some boxers and loose slacks, he climbed into bed on top of the covers.

As he began to fall asleep from physical and emotional exhaustion, his mind still refused to shut down. The last thing he remembered thinking is: "This time it will be different. This time I'll catch him before he can destroy me."

7:15 p.m.

Walking into the kitchen through the backdoor, The Surgeon was clearly upset. He had regained control of his anger, but this new development still made his blood boil. Hoping to find Chicanery at home, he walked into the living room to find it empty, but with the TV on some kind of cop drama. Hearing movement in the master bedroom, he headed that way.

Nonchalantly entering his employers' bedroom, he exclaims angrily, "Why didn't you tell me he was here? You played me, motherfucker."

Turning briskly, enraged by this intrusion, Chicanery says, "Who the fuck do you think you are? I told you never to come back here. You are allowed in the kitchen or the hideaway. Get the fuck out of here."

"Not till you answer the question."

"I do not know who you are referring to. As for playing you, of course I did. We both played each other to get what we wanted out of this business deal. You money. Me chaos. Now leave."

"I'm referring to St. James. You knew who I was talking about, asshole."

"Oh, him. Fine, so what if I withheld my knowledge of him. I didn't feel it would help you on the job. In fact, I felt getting the upper hand was more important. Now go to the kitchen before someone sees you. I'll be there shortly."

Growling like a wolf, The Surgeon walked out the door and headed toward the kitchen, mumbling to himself the entire way. Grabbing a beer from the fridge, he sat at the kitchen table and waited. After taking a long pull on the bottle of Michelob, he looked up to find Chicanery walking through the entryway.

"If you ever invade my privacy again, I will kill you, do I make myself clear?"

"Perfectly," The Surgeon replied sarcastically.

"Whatever. Now about St. James, he was never a priority for you. He's just a bonus. Getting him back wasn't why I contacted you. The job was why I did. And unfortunately for my pocketbook, I can't let you stop with the mission yet."

"What do you mean? I want fucking St. James."

"And you can have him when this is over. Don't you want some fun with him first though? I mean, you're getting paid, and in the end, you can kill St. James."

Stopping to take some deep breaths, and to consider his angle with this new information, The Surgeon began to smile to himself. After a few minutes he looked up and replied, "Sure, I could use more money for my retirement plan. Just don't play me for a fool again."

"No problem, man."

"Okay, what's the new job?"

A half hour later, The Surgeon found himself in his hideaway looking at the blueprints to his new objective. After committing the entire layout to memory, he sat back to plan. This job wouldn't be complicated, as long as someone didn't get away again. He would deal with the girl later. For now, the message he was sending should suffice.

Lying back in bed, he smiled as he reflected on how he would kill not only St. James, but his employer as well.

Chapter 8

Remembering

Saturday, May 13
7:22 a.m.

Kiara woke up from her drug-induced slumber to find her dad had fallen asleep at bedside holding her hand. Her mother was asleep in a chair behind him. Evidently, they hadn't left last night, and had somehow convinced the hospital to allow them to stay.

Trying not to disturb her father, she carefully removed his hand, so she could get out of bed. Going to the bathroom, she returned to find her mother stretching and yawning. Trying to sound as cheerful and pain free as possible, she said, "Morning, mom."

"Morning sweetie. How are you feeling?"

"Still a little groggy from the medication, and sore from the wreck, but otherwise okay."

"That's nice. Are you hungry? I can go see if breakfast will be served soon, if you want."

"That's okay, I can just push this button," holding up the call switch from the bed, "and you won't even have to get up."

At this point, her dad began stirring, looked up and said, "What are you doing out of bed, honey? You need to relax."

"The doctor did say I could go to the bathroom on my own, Dad. Otherwise, I'd still have that tube thingy in place. Stop worrying, I'm fine."

"Just get back in bed, please. It'll ease my mind at least."

Getting back in bed, she allowed her father to tuck her back in, then pushed the call button. In a brief moment, the nurse bustled her way in, and asked "Is everything okay? What do you need?"

"I was just hoping to get some breakfast. Do you know when that will get here?" she responded.

"You woke up just in time. They just began their second rounds with breakfast trays. Let me see if I can find yours for you, dear."

Her mother spoke up at this point, "Ted, could you run down to the cafeteria and see if you can get us something to eat? We're not the patient. They're not gonna provide for us, too."

"Sure, Margarette," then, getting up to leave, "Just make sure Kiara takes care while I'm gone."

"She'll be fine, now go."

Watching her dad walk out of the room, Kiara shook her head. Sometimes her dad was way overprotective. She loved him though.

Looking at her mother, she said, "Were you able to get a hold of Daniel for me? Will I see him later?"

"We were unable to get through on the telephone last night. For some reason the line was busy every time we tried. It was probably that he was trying to call you. We'll keep trying, honey, and if we don't hear soon I'll have your dad go over there."

"Okay, Mom, thanks," she said.

Grabbing the TV remote, she began flipping through the channels to pass the time. While she was looking for a program, the nurse brought in her breakfast.

"Now I know it's not much, but we want to make sure your body can handle food before giving you too much. Try to eat everything, and if you feel nauseated at all let us know, okay?"

"Okay."

The meal was definitely meager. It consisted of a portion of scrambled egg, one slice of unbuttered toast, and a bowl of unsweetened, mushy looking oatmeal. For a beverage they gave her hot tea and apple juice.

Oh well, at least it was something, she thought to herself. Continuing to flip through the channels as she picked at her breakfast, she paused on the morning news when she saw body bags being removed from a familiar restaurant.

"As you can see from the camera footage on screen, we are looking at one of the bodies from Izzolio's Restaurant as it is being taken to a nearby coroner's van. This is still our top story from yesterday as we continue to unravel the mysteries behind this multiple homicide scene . . . "

The story continued to unfold, but Kiara had already lost track of what was being said. Her mind was conjuring up memories of before the accident that she didn't want to believe were true. She heard someone screaming, and thought she could hear her mother trying to speak soothingly to her. Suddenly she felt hands grabbing her body, and she reacted.

Trying to twist and turn to keep whoever was grabbing her from being able to do so, she realized she was the one screaming. Coming back to reality, she saw two male nurses trying to restrain her while another nurse attempted to give her a shot and her mother stood off in the corner, wide-eyed. She felt the needle prick her arm and the last thing she remembered seeing, were tears falling from her mother's eyes.

5:28 a.m. (same day)

In a flash he had his Glock in his hand and pointed at the door. "Don't move," he yelled. The silhouette in his bedroom doorway jumped.

"Don't shoot, Mark, it's just me," the soft sound of Rebecca's voice responded.

Sighing with relief, he put his gun down on the night stand and said, "Goddamn, Becky, do you realize how close you were to ending up on your own autopsy table?"

"I'm sorry. I knocked several times with no response. I started getting worried about you, so I used the key you gave me for emergencies." Stepping up to his bed, she noticed tears running down his face, "Oh, Mark. They started again, didn't they?" Lifting her hand up to his face, she delicately wiped the tears away.

Slightly embarrassed, and realizing how vulnerable he was to her right now, especially with an exposed chest and obvious morning woody showing, he jumped out of bed. Moving toward the bedroom door, he responded, "I told you at the office I'd survive. I'm not as weak as I was three years ago, Becky. I haven't broken my promise, either, if that's what you're worried about."

Watching him walk toward the bathroom, she was amazed by his shyness sometimes. He had such an awesome, muscular body. Sometimes she didn't think he realized what he did to her. Her body shivered as she felt warmth and wetness in her womanhood. God, she wanted him sometimes. Feeling her face begin to flush, she tried changing her thoughts by saying, "I didn't come here because I was worried about that. I came here because Kidd called me and asked me to check in with you after you didn't answer the phone."

"Oh, well, that's probably because I turned it off to get some much-needed rest," he said from behind the bathroom door. "What did Kidd want?"

"Apparently they found Kiara. You'll have to get a hold of her for details. She just told me to check in on you and tell you 'found the witness, call me.' So how bad was it? You can stop the act with me."

"I told you I'm fine. My eyes were just watering from lack of sleep."

"Hmph. That's a crock of shit and we both know it."

"Stop pushing me, Becky. I will talk to you when I need to."

"Fine. Just don't shut me out, Mark. I love you," she blurted out in anger. She could hear something drop into the sink and then nothing.

The silence seemed to last forever. Finally, the bathroom door opened and he stepped into the bedroom fully dressed minus the shoes and socks, then sat on the bed and began to put them on. Looking at her, he said, "Listen, I'm sorry. I promise if things get too difficult, we'll talk. All it is is nightmares. Unless you have a non-addictive prescription, there isn't much else we can do."

"I'm sorry, too, Mark. I just worry is all, and these new murders have put me on edge."

"Hey, don't go anywhere, okay. I'll cook us some breakfast when I get done talking to Kidd."

"Alright, I'll get the coffee started."

As she began leaving, he cleared his throat, and said, slightly uncomfortable, "Hey Becky, listen, about what you said before, the love part that is, you know I care about you, a lot, right? It's just…I miss Susan, especially now."

"Mark, don't worry about it. It was just something I blurted out." Walking out the door, she felt a tear shed down her cheek.

Watching her leave, he felt bad. He knew he had handled the last part badly. Going to the bathroom, he took his cell out and dialed Kidd's home number. After about eight rings he heard her groggily say, "Kidd here."

"It's me. What's up?"

"Kiara Benson has been located, but there's a problem."

"What's that?"

"She's a patient at the Q.M.C. Apparently she was in a car accident on the night of the murders. The story is hazy, but it looks like while running from the scene she ran into the street and got hit by oncoming traffic. The problem isn't that, though. Her parents and doctor have stonewalled Stintz and Jon. They claim she doesn't remember anything and she isn't medically stable."

"How much truth is there to the story? Are her parents just being protective?"

"No, I believe them because I knew Dr. Louise Moore and talked with her personally. I believe the child is stable and has amnesia. Stintz has been trying to get me to call the judge for a warrant. I've been stalling him because I thought a more conventional means would be appropriate."

"I see where you're going with this and the answer is no. I'm not on the force anymore and you can't order me to do it."

"My point exactly. Being a P.I., removes you from the suspicions of the family. The girl is going to need protection from now on, and who better to do it than you? With your experience in the military and in the force you're the perfect man for the job. It might even get some money your way."

"Fine Kidd, but you owe me."

"Good, I knew I could count on you. She's in room 212."

"I'll talk to you when I'm in. Bye, Kidd."

Shutting his cell, he left the bedroom and walked down the hallway toward the kitchen. Walking through the entryway, he found Rebecca had coffee going and breakfast started. "What can I do to help?" he asked.

"Chop the ham, peppers, and onions up. Then shred the cheese."

While he started that, he watched her scramble the eggs in a bowl and put bacon in the frying pan. For a moment he saw Susan standing there with him again, but then he remembered she was gone. Swallowing the lump rising in his throat, he began chopping the vegetables.

Chapter 9

Assignments

Saturday, May 13
10:06 a.m.

Arriving at the hospital, Mark was in a splendid mood. Breakfast with Rebecca had ended up being perfect, despite the conversation in his bedroom. Somehow, she always ended up brightening his day. She truly did have a heart of gold.

Walking through reception, he approached the front desk and asked if Dr. Louise Moore was available.

"May I ask who's inquiring sir?" the receptionist responded.

"Mark St. James, P.I."

"Sure, wait just one moment while I try her extension, please."

Turning his back and looking around the room, he noticed all of the sick people. There were about a dozen people of varying ages sitting in the waiting room. An elderly couple were sitting in one corner. The husband was confined to his wheelchair, and appeared to be dealing with the later stages of Alzheimer's. His wife was whispering to him in comforting tones. To Mark's left, a young child was coloring pictures on a coffee table while her mother leafed through a Woman's Day magazine, periodically glancing her daughter's way. He watched as the little girl occasionally coughed up mucus into a Kleenex she'd grabbed from a nearby box. Wondering how many would survive the year or even the month, he realized just how out of touch he was with other people. Ever since his family had died, he was afraid to get too close to people. It was hard to allow himself to become vulnerable.

"Excuse me, sir."

Turning around to face the receptionist he replied, "Yes."

"I was unable to get through to her. I can page her if you'd like."

"Please, this is about an important matter. If she arrives before I return, please let her know I'll be in the gift shop."

Heading toward the gift shop, he still felt slightly guilty about his exchange with Rebecca, despite how well breakfast had gone. Walking into the Q.M.C. Gift Shoppe, he headed toward the flower section.

"How much are your roses?" he asked an employee at the counter.

"Six and a quarter per stem. There's a special as well, you can get half a dozen with balloons for $35."

"One will be fine. Please place it in a vase and attach a card that says 'Sorry, thanks for a wonderful breakfast.' Forward it to Ms. Hall's office. Thanks." Turning around, a woman in her mid-thirties stood before him. She was slightly shorter than he, with close-cropped red hair lying around her neck. She had light blue eyes, dimples, and a ready smile. Wearing a doctor's smock over jeans and a blue blouse, she looked quite attractive.

"Are you Mr. St. James?" she asked.

"Yes, you must be Dr. Moore,"

"I am. The receptionist told me you had some important matters to discuss."

"I do. I'm here in regards to a Ms. Kiara Benson. I'm told she's a patient of yours."

"She is, however due to patient/doctor confidentiality I cannot discuss her case without a court order."

"No problem. I'm not here for that. I'm here to let you know your patient's life is in danger and to offer my assistance. I don't know if you are fully aware of the situation."

"Yes, as a matter of fact I am," she interrupted, "Chief Kidd has already placed an officer outside Kiara's door. Besides, due to recent complications with the patient I don't think it would be a good idea to see her."

"Why, what happened?"

"All I'm at liberty to say is that she is resting after being given a sedative from having an emotional reaction to the morning news special about the multiple homicide two nights ago."

"I believe at this point it is even more important to tighten security on Ms. Benson. If she remembers anything after this morning, she is even more of a threat to the killer."

"Look Mr. St. James, you may plead your case with the parents, but I'm with them. Whatever they decide you'll have to do."

"Fine, thanks for your help, doctor."

Paying for the gift and walking out, he headed in the direction of the elevators. Taking a elevator up to the second floor, he stepped out and began looking for room 212. Passing by several rooms with sick patients in them, he saw an assortment of people enduring various stages of illnesses. In one room, a couple of adolescents appeared to be consoling an injured teammate, while in another room a woman in her fifties was puking into a bed pan. Making a stop at the nurses' station, he asked where 212 was located and, following the directions, found Officer Bruce Cavets sitting outside the door.

"Hey Mark, how are you," he greeted.

"Good. Are the parents in?"

"Yeah, and the girl is still out. I'll tell you one thing, she's a strong one. It took four orderlies to hold her for the shot earlier."

"Could have just been adrenaline, Bruce. Can I go in?"

"Yeah, the Chief called and told me I'd be seeing you."

"Thanks, I'll see you in a minute."

Knocking on the door and then strolling in, he saw a standard patient room with a young lady asleep in the bed, while the mother and father sat opposite one another on either side of the hospital bed. The father looked to be in his early forties, with slightly tanned skin and hairy arms. He looked tired and worn out. His dark brown eyes, saddened by worry, were blood shot from lack of sleep and crying. Her mother was about the same age, had a creamy tone to her skin as if she didn't go out in the sun often, and had light green eyes. She looked just as tired and emotionally overwhelmed as her husband.

"Sorry for interrupting. My name is Mark St. James. I'm a private investigator and consultant to the Q.P.D. on the case you daughter is involved in."

"We've already told the police our daughter is in no condition to answer questions," the father stated.

"You misunderstand, Mr. Benson. I'm not here on behalf of the Q.P.D., or to ask questions. I'm here to express to you the seriousness of this situation. Two nights ago, a brutal killer murdered twenty-eight men, women and children. It appears your daughter may have been the only witness. Originally when your daughter had amnesia, she was a minimal risk to the killer. Now she is an extreme risk to him. Therefore, I would like to request to assist you in her safety."

"We understand the risk, but we don't have a lot of money. We couldn't ever afford private security."

"That's no problem. My only concern is Kiara's safety. I'll wave all fees, till later. We can discuss payment after we get through this, that is."

Looking at his wife before responding, he asked, "Well what are we talking about here?"

"I would make myself available as additional security for Kiara until the killer is caught. I know several veterans on the force whom I trust with my life. I will call them and I'm sure I can convince them to help me out. In the meantime, I do need to know what you know."

"Fine."

And with that, Mr. and Mrs. Benson began telling him everything that had happened since Thursday night.

1:07 p.m.

The Surgeon surveyed every aspect of the environment. After being contacted by his source in the Q.P.D. he knew he had to check security out at the hospital. From everything he'd seen so far, it was minimal.

Scaring this family into making a mistake so he could kill them wouldn't be a problem. The location of their deaths would be more difficult. He would have to kill this witness; the parents were just an added bonus.

Stopping several feet from room 212, when he saw St. James step out and talk to the officer outside the door, he found himself imagining momentarily how he planned to kill this man. Continuing down the hall and watching St. James pull out his cell to make a call, The Surgeon shivered with adrenaline from how close he was to being caught. These men were such fools. He was so good he could walk right past them and spit on their shoes without being arrested. The thought brought a smile to his face. Making eye contact with St. James briefly, he nodded and kept walking.

St. James just made things interesting. He was going to enjoy killing this family right under St. James' nose. He could feel the rush run through his veins as he adjusted his plans to fit St. James into them.

CHAPTER 10

REUNIONS

Sunday, May 14
6:08 p.m.

Her father knocked on the room door, stuck his head in, and said, "Look who I found wandering the hallways." Pushing the door all the way open, he stepped aside to reveal Daniel's parents and little sister standing outside. They all had their best smiles of comfort on them as they walked into the room. Rachelle ran up to the bed, vaulted the railing, and planted her face on Kiara's shoulder, then began to cry. Shirley and Daniel Sr. came over and patted her legs comfortingly, both trying for all the world to appear strong.

She burst into tears as she once again faced the reality of everyone's loss. Did they know he had planned on marrying her? Did they blame her for being alive while their son was dead? It appeared they did not, but would she ever know the truth?

"Mr. and Mrs. Verin, it's very good to see all of you again," she blurted out, then began sobbing.

"Yes, it's good to see you again, too, dear. Sorry we didn't come sooner, but your parents felt it best to wait till your memory returned, or until we could find a way to break the news safely to you," Mr. Verin replied.

"Yeah, I know. Although I'm still upset at them for lying to me, I understand why they did," she said, briefly glancing at her parents.

"C'mon Rachelle, that's enough crying now, baby. Kiara needs her body back. It's still pretty banged up," Mrs. Verin told her daughter.

Looking up and wiping tears from her eyes, Rachelle said, "Sorry KiKi, but I couldn't hold it in. I miss DanDan so bad."

"Yeah, me too, sweetheart," she replies, patting her on the back.

For the next half hour everyone exchanged pleasantries and tried to be strong for the others as they talked about the last week. Mark St. James looked in on them briefly to make sure everything was okay and to tell them he'd be back in the morning. Soon after that, she finally asked, "When is Daniel's funeral?"

"The M.E. is releasing Daniel tomorrow. On Wednesday, there will be a memorial for all the victims. Thursday we'll bury him. We hope you will be able to be there," Mr. Verin said.

"I understand. I'll try to be there, I'm sure. Did you know he proposed to me that night?"

The Verins looked at one another, then Mrs. Verin finally began crying as she said, "Oh Kiara, we're so sorry. Yes, we knew he was planning on it, but we didn't know if he'd done it before everything went wrong."

As she opened her arms to invite Mrs. Verin in, they embraced and held onto one another for a while, allowing each other to mourn. After a few minutes, Mrs. Verin pulled away, and said, while blotting tears from her eyes with a Kleenex, "Daniel was a good boy. I know you both would have been very happy together."

"I loved him with all my heart, Mrs. Verin. I just wish I wouldn't have run to the restroom when he proposed instead of answering him. It's my fault he's dead. Maybe if I had responded immediately, we would have left before everyone died," she cried out.

"Nonsense Kiara, it wasn't your fault. You mustn't blame yourself. Besides if you had been with him, you'd be dead, too. And call me Shirley, you were practically family, and will be considered as so from now on."

"I just can't help replaying it over and over again in my head. I keep rewinding and telling myself if I'd done it differently Daniel would still be here."

"Calm down, honey. Let's place the blame where it belongs, on the monster who did this. Besides, from what I've been told, we need to keep you safe for now. So, let's just concentrate on that," Mr. Verin consoled.

Blowing her nose and nodding, she said, "Thank you Mr. Verin, Shirley. Thank you both."

The rest of the evening was spent watching TV, playing cards, and talking about everything except that night and the loss of Daniel. Around nine o'clock the Verins left so they could put Rachelle to bed. Her mom went home to shower, leaving her dad and the cop outside to watch over her.

As everyone settled down for the night, Kiara still couldn't stop replaying that night in her head, and wondered why she was still alive.

6:30 p.m.

The hospital cafeteria was painted an awful puke green. He'd never understood what was so comforting about institutional colors like mellow yellow, standard white, or the present color of this cafeteria, but evidently someone else did. The rest of the cafeteria was set up with a serving line and salad bar as you entered, and plenty of tables partitioned by a long flower bed.

He'd come down from the Benson's room for a short coffee break. The room was still being covered by the Q.P.D., so he didn't need to be there anyway. The family was very close and loving. Mr. Benson was a bit too overprotective, but with everything that had happened he had a right to be. Besides he had been a father too, and understood, all too well, how a father felt about his children. His daughter had been his world, and his son had been the best little tyke a guy could want.

The Bensons were a kind and caring bunch, but being around them was difficult. They constantly brought forth memories of his own family. The danger Kiara was in only amplified his feelings of personal loss. He needed this break for a little while.

Returning to his thoughts on the case, he considered the new evidence Rebecca told him on the phone last night. The toxicology screen results found only one anomaly in all the victims. The victims' blood was laced with Latrodectus, more commonly known as black widow venom. This explained the paralysis, but he was still baffled about how it had been introduced to the victims. For that matter, he still wanted to know where the killer had come up with enough to dose an entire restaurant. It was definitely a good lead, and apparently what the killer commonly used.

"Mark, is that really you?"

He looked up to find a tall, muscular black man standing next to his table. The man looked vaguely familiar, but he couldn't place where he'd seen him before. "Yes, and you are?"

"It's me, David Nixxon. C'mon, don't tell me you've forgotten about one of your old Navy recruits."

"Oh, yeah, Nixxon. You were one of my best students. Hey, sorry about giving you such a hard time, but you gotta admit it paid off. You probably never would have finished in the top five if I hadn't."

"No problem, it's water under the bridge. Besides you were just doing your job."

"Yeah, so what brings you to the town of Quincy?"

"My uncle is being treated for Hodgkin's. My aunt and uncle have lived here for about ten years or so now. They found out he had the disease about a year ago. We were really close when I was growing up and they lived in Baltimore. Thought I'd come down and show some support for a few days," he explained.

"Oh, sorry to hear that, son. How is he?"

"He's doing fine. The doctors claim he'll live. He may need to be treated the rest of his life, but he's in good health otherwise, so he might be cured."

"That's good."

Nixxon nodded and smiled, then asked, "So, what are you doing here?"

"I'm a P.I. now, and one of my clients is a patient here."

"A P.I., hmm. Not the job I'd have pegged for you all those years ago."

"It has its perks. I get to have my own hours and catch bad guys. Wouldn't have it any other way."

"Well, it was nice seeing you again. Maybe we can catch a beer at the tavern and reminisce on old times sometime."

"I'd love to catch up again, but I'll have to pass on the beer. My office number is in the Yellow Pages. Call me."

"Got it. See you later, Mark."

Watching him leave, Mark reflected briefly on his Navy days. He still had a lot of connections from those times. Being in the Navy was one of the defining moments of his life.

Returning to his new case, he began considering all of the factors which played into the killer's psyche. As he got up from the table and started listing the characteristics, he had to change his original assessment. He wasn't dealing with your average serial killer. This one seemed to have intelligence and a purpose. A very lethal combination.

Chapter 11

A Message Delivered

Monday, May 15
11:22 a.m.

Mark stood outside of the MRI room in the Neurology Department. He wasn't the sitting patiently type. He preferred standing when he could, because it allowed free movement. The ability to move quickly was required in his line of duty, so he found it more comfortable to just stand.

Glancing down the hall, he could see Mr. and Mrs. Benson pacing in the waiting room. He knew very soon he would have to discuss security precautions regarding their daughter with them, but for now he wanted to supervise his client's testing. It's not that he didn't trust the Q.P.D. officers, it was just that he didn't want to lose this one.

Kiara was a sweetheart. She was a strong, vibrant young woman who deserved to live. He intended to see that she did. He could not imagine going through what she had and continuing to maintain a lick of sanity. She seemed to have just that though.

Thinking of her made him think about his daughter. Molly would have been eight this year. She was such an innocent little girl. She had the most beautiful smile; it could charm the hell out of him, no matter whether she had been right or wrong. Once again, he found this line of thinking distressing. In just a short couple of weeks, it would be three years since he had lost his family. He couldn't focus on that right now, though.

Forcing his attention back to the here and now, he noticed a man down the hallway, walking around. He'd seen him several times before. He appeared to be monitoring this area from a distance. He was short, stocky, and appeared to be in his late thirties. He had red hair, wore glasses, and had on white nurse's scrubs. Mark's gut told him something was wrong with this character, so pretending to grab his phone to take a call, he pressed the three and send buttons quickly, as he brought the phone to his ear. He really enjoyed this feature in his cell, because it allowed him to make quick calls without a potential suspect knowing what he was doing.

Acting like he said something, then waiting for the chief to pick up, like he was listening to a response, was second nature to him now, he'd done it quite often in situations like this. After two rings Kidd picked up and said, "Yeah, Mark."

"Kidd would you call the reception area outside Kiara's room and tell them to send Matthews down here to relieve me for a few minutes?"

"Sure, but why don't you just do it yourself?"

"Because I'm watching a possible suspect and don't want to tip him off," he responded, patronizingly.

"No need to be abrupt, I'll get it done," she said angrily.

"Thanks, and Kidd I'm sorry. I'm just not used to people questioning my authority yet."

"Yeah, yeah, just be careful and don't shoot anybody."

Clipping the phone back to his belt, he waited outside the MRI, periodically glancing around and watching for the short red head. Just a few minutes before Matthews showed up, the man appeared again. Unobtrusively explaining the situation to

Matthews, Mark left him on guard duty and walked toward the doors. He headed to an observation post so he could watch for the short man again.

After waiting about ten minutes he showed up again. Mark watched him as he tried to inconspicuously observe the hallway Kiara's MRI was taking place in. Every few seconds he would nervously rub his hands together. A few minutes later the man walked away, and he followed.

Following him down several hallways, the man ended up outside the hospital's employee lounge, which he walked into. Looking both ways and seeing no one looking, he went in after the man. Entering the room, he found the man sitting on a couch, looking at the floor, wringing his hands together.

Walking over to him, he asked, "Are you okay, sir?"

The man looked up at him with a clearly worried face, he responded, "Huh, yeah I'm fine. Who are you? What are you doing in here? I've never seen you in here before. Are you an employee?"

"No, my name is Mark St. James. I'm a P.I. watching over a client who is a patient here."

"So, what are you doing in here talking to me?"

"I noticed you have been frequently watching down the hallway my client has been getting tests done in, so I wanted to check things out. You looked very suspicious at the time. May I see some I.D.?"

"No, you may not. I'm just an employee of this hospital who's worried about his wife, if you don't mind."

"Listen, sir, I'm sorry, but I really do need to see some ID. It's just for security purposes."

"Hey fuck you, buddy. This is a free country. I don't need to show you a god damn thing. You're not even a cop."

Reaching for his phone to call hospital security he replied, "I'm afraid I'm gonna have to call hospital security to confirm who you are."

Getting up from the couch, the man said, "Like hell."

Unsure what the man's intentions were, Mark immediately grabbed his wrist, twisted him around, and restrained his arm behind his back.

Struggling, the man cried out, "What the fuck's wrong with you, man? Get off me."

Just as he began dialing the hospital's security number on his cell, another man entered the lounge. Seeing the tussle, his eyes widened and he yells angrily, "What the hell is happening here? Let go of Dale. What do you think you're doing? I'm calling security." The man moved toward the door to leave.

"Wait," Mark exclaimed, and the man paused, then looked back at him fearfully. "Do you know this man?"

"Yes, that's nurse Davies. Why are you restraining him?"

Releasing the man, he began apologizing and trying to talk his way out of a lawsuit.

12:05 p.m.

Walking back to the MRI room, he felt embarrassed, foolish, and frustrated all at the same time. After some clever, smooth talking and a hundred-dollar bill, he had managed to keep the misunderstanding under wraps, but he still felt angry--more with himself than anyone else. Turning onto the hallway he'd been on, he found Kiara was just getting done with the test. A nurse was pushing her down the hallway in a wheelchair, as Matthews followed. Stopping, Mark waited for them to reach him, then smiled at Kiara and asked, "So, how'd it go?

"Don't know, the doctor said the results should be back by supper."

Walking into the waiting area with her, he watched as her parents approached with concerned looks on their faces. They discussed briefly how the test went, and then the nurse began walking everyone toward the elevator. Getting on the elevator and going up two floors, they got out and headed toward room 212.

Entering Kiara's room, the nurse began to get her out of the chair and back into bed. After telling the nurse she wanted to go to the bathroom, the nurse let her go and told her to get back in bed afterwards. Watching Kiara head toward the bathroom and flip the light switch on, Mark jumped when a piercing scream vibrated throughout the room.

Running to her side, just seconds before her parents and the nurse, he glimpsed a horrid sight as he pulled her away from the doorway. Handing her over to her parents, he took his cell from his pocket as he glanced back into the hospital bathroom.

A look of disgust and amazement appeared on his face as he stared at the blood smeared words *Don't tell a soul* on the mirror. And if that weren't a clear enough message, sitting in the sink was a bloody tongue.

CHAPTER 12

HOMECOMING

Monday, May 15
8:06 p.m.

The last eight hours seemed to have passed in a blur for her. The drugs the nurses had given her after the last panic attack, made her mind hazy and slow. She remembered blood dripping down the bathroom mirror and the grotesque tongue sitting in the sink. The words of warning were still seen on the back of her eyelids each time she closed them. Everything else had happened too fast for her to process it all.

The shot they gave her knocked her out almost immediately. She came around several times to hear Mr. St. James talking quietly with her parents, arguing with her doctor, or talking on the telephone in hushed tones. Her parents had concerned expressions on their faces when looking at her. Everyone appeared to be putting themselves fully into protecting her. Unfortunately, everyone wanted it done differently.

When unconscious, she dreamt. Her dreams were erratic and overwhelming. At one point she awoke feeling sea sick and realized she was in a car on the road to somewhere, then she floated off to oblivion again.

Stretching and blinking her eyes, she came back to reality to find herself lying in her own bed at home. Her bedroom had been cleaned and straightened up. Her mother probably did it while she was in the hospital. Looking around, she jumped slightly when she saw Mr. St. James sitting in an arm chair near her. He appeared to be sleeping. She couldn't tell for sure, though, so she tried to get up quietly to go pee.

"No need for silence, I'm not sleeping," a voice from the chair spoke.

"Sorry, Mr. St. James. You looked like you were sleeping. I didn't want to wake you," she responded. Leaving the room and going across the hall, she sat on the toilet. Cleaning up, she went back to her bedroom. "So, Mr. St. James, what are we going to do now?"

"Well, our main objective is to keep you safe until we catch this man. In order to do this, you will need to make some adjustments in your life."

"What kind of adjustments?"

"First of all, there will be two non-uniformed officers everywhere you go. You will need to allow them to check every room you go into before you enter it, and your privacy will be affected. Fortunately, your daily schedule can remain the same for the most part. Do you think you can do this?"

"I don't know, I'm really scared. At this point I don't even know if I want to leave the house."

"I understand. I plan on being with you as much as possible, but the killer seems to have some interest in me as well, so I may have to leave you to the regular Q.P.D. force occasionally. I promise you, though, only the people I trust in the force will be with you. I'm assuming you'll still want to attend the memorial on Wednesday. Am I right?"

"Of course. I'm not gonna let my fear stop me from saying goodbye to Daniel."

"I thought so. Everything has been arranged for your attendance, and unless you want to go somewhere you can relax till then as well. Your parents spoke to the school, and you don't have to go tomorrow. I wanted to be here when you woke up to tell you about all this personally and answer any questions you may have. I will be going home soon, but I'll check on you later."

"I understand, Mr. St. James. I guess my only question is what do we do if you can't catch him. I don't want to feel scared the rest of my life."

"You let us worry about that, and I promise you we will catch him. I won't allow another killer to win again," St. James replied angrily.

"Are you okay, sir?"

"Yeah, I've just been doing this for a while. Your parents are in the living room if you need them. I'll talk to you later, Kiara. Also, you should know for the time being there will be a couple of officers in a car out front, and one inside the house at all times. If you have any problems, they're here."

"Okay. Talk to you later Mr. St. James."

Watching him get up and leave her bedroom, she suddenly felt more vulnerable.

8:31 p.m.

"Your daughter is awake and has been apprised of the situation," he said to the Bensons, as he entered the living room. Mr. Benson was sitting on the couch holding his wife, who had been crying, whispering to her. "Excuse me, sir, I'm very sorry for walking in like this, I'll come back in a few minutes," Mark stated, embarrassed at his actions.

"No, you're fine. We are going to have to get used to this for now, anyway," Mr. Benson responded. "So, how is she doing?"

Turning back into the living room and taking a seat on the lounge chair, he said, "She's a strong girl, but she's also scared out of her mind. She's gonna need a lot of comfort and support for a while. Also, if I may suggest, a therapist would help out immensely. I can suggest someone if you'd like."

Looking at her husband, Mrs. Benson replied, "That would be fine, but we don't know what to do. We are just as scared as our daughter. Why is the man doing this?"

"He is afraid your daughter saw more than she has, so he considers her a threat. Even though we know all she saw was a shadow, the killer can't take the risk she'll identify him. I'm very sorry this has happened to you."

"We just can't believe it's really happening. This feels like a nightmare we can't get ourselves to wake up from," Mrs. Benson exclaimed.

"Believe me, if anyone understands about nightmares it's me," he said, sorrowfully. "For now just keep an eye on her, and remember to utilize the officers here. If you need me, you know how to contact me. I'll see you tomorrow."

"Thank you, Mr. St. James."

Getting up, he walked to the front door, passing by officer Clarks on the way. As he left, he told the officers out front to keep him informed. Breathing a loud sigh of relief as he pulled away from the house, he wondered what the new day had in store for all of them.

CHAPTER 13

MEMORIALS

Wednesday, May 17
1:33 p.m.

Walking around the scene, while trying to keep his eye on Kiara, he found it hard not to feel depressed. There had to be close to a hundred town residents in attendance. So many forced to mourn the loss of loved ones. So many lost to the hands of a sadistic killer.

He was hard pressed to maintain focus on the situation at hand. Memories of his own loss continued to flood his mind. It had been two hours since his arrival with the Bensons. Two hours of trying to block the memories so he could do his job effectively.

The memorial service was being held on the courthouse lawn. It was decided this would be the best spot because of proximity of the town's churches, parking capabilities and space. It was also a good spot for its beauty. Surrounding the lawn were sycamore, oak, pine, and maple trees. Flowers of all sorts and kinds were displayed wondrously across the lawn. Lilies, chrysanthemums, tulips, hyacinths, irises, daffodils, crocuses, and bougainvilleas as well as an assortment of berry bushes were sprawled magnificently around the expanse of the field around the courthouse. This calm spring day only enhanced the beauty of Mother Nature. It was about 65 degrees, a slight cool breeze waved its way between the trees and lawn, and the sky only had a few wisps of clouds.

Despite all of this, the general atmosphere was gloomy and sad. Pictures of the twenty-eight victims were spread out on easels around the area. Family and friends congregated in the vicinity of those they knew. Due to the circumstances and the overwhelming number of children in attendance, school had been closed for the service.

The sounds of crying, sniffling, and moaning could be heard behind all the quiet whispering and condolences. It was all very disheartening. Looking around, he felt stabs of sympathy and pain for all in attendance. Having experienced what they were now feeling only intensified his empathy for everyone here. He caught a glimpse of Rebecca walking his way, as he turned to face Kiara again.

Stopping at his side, she said, "It's just so frustrating. The unfairness of it all. I sometimes wonder at the cruelty of human suffering. Where is God in all of this?"

"I ask myself the same thing, Becky. That's the question I've asked myself for three years. I still don't have an answer. Apparently, He isn't listening, or wants us to wait longer for the answer. How are you doing?"

"I'm okay. I came to support the people here. Being the one who handled all of these cases in one form or another, I felt it was important to try and support all of those who survived their loved ones." Looking at him, their eyes connecting, she said with meaning, "Even after all of the random and purposeful acts of violence over the years, I still have a heavy heart when I face the living. Does it ever get easier?"

"No, not really. I've seen death in combat, as a cop, and now as a P.I., for the last 20 years and it still feels like a sledgehammer across my chest when I look at these people."

Nodding at each other, they stood in silence, just comforting one another by their mere presence as they monitored the memorial.

2:02 p.m.

Looking down at the crowd through the scope of his SR-25 rifle, he stalked Kiara and the rest of his intended victims. The room he sat in was dark and barely furnished. The Surgeon sat in a chair, wearing a black nylon suit by the window. The clothes he'd come in with were sitting on the floor beside him.

On a stand beside him was a joystick-like controller, similar to those used to control the military's Predator drones. Adjusting the controller slightly, he returned to looking through the scope and watched Kiara as she spoke with another student. She was just barely maintaining her composure, not crying although he'd witnessed many tears already this day. Smiling to himself, he waited for the reactions to begin.

2:06 p.m.

Listening to Rebecca, Mark glanced at Kiara briefly and began to look back at Rebecca, when it dawned on him what he'd seen. Quickly looking back at Kiara to confirm what he saw, he immediately sprinted toward her, pushing several innocent bystanders out of his way. He could hear Rebecca saying, "Mark, what's going on?" as he left her side.

Moving like he was a NFL running back, he jumped and tackled Kiara as the first screams began. Looking up, he saw several people going down as if they were fainting from sorrow. Checking to make sure Kiara was okay, he told her to stay down, then yelled at the two officers in the area to radio for help.

Everyone was either scattering in all directions, or on the ground screaming. It was chaos. Grabbing his cell he dialed 911, then called Kidd and told her to seal off the courthouse—the laser sight had been coming from there. Glancing toward where Rebecca had been with him, he didn't see her there. Looking around, he saw her sprawled on the ground, not moving.

2:15 p.m.

Taking apart the rifle and placing it in the briefcase quickly, The Surgeon was disappointed. He had failed to meet his objective. The woman was still alive, and he knew he had to get out. Scanning the area for evidence, he efficiently cleaned everything up and put his clothing on.

Leaving the area quietly, he walked briefcase in hand to the end of the hallway, taking a right and heading to the elevators. Taking the elevator down, he entered the lobby and, whistling, left the building. Watching the results of his actions, he chuckled at the pandemonium as he leisurely walked away.

Chapter 14

Chaos and Loss

Wednesday, May 17
2:20 p.m.

Running back toward Rebecca, Mark stopped and dropped to his knees by her side. Blood was running freely from her head. Fearfully, he pulled her into his arms and checked for a pulse. She had one, and he breathed a sigh of relief.

Examining her head, he found a gash running from her temple to just behind her ear. She was alive! She'd gotten lucky, but she would make it. Feeling tears staining the sides of his cheeks, he held her until the paramedic arrived.

At some point Kiara had come and sat by his side. Her parents kept trying to get her to come with them, and he even told her to go with them, but she refused. He let her stay, and made sure a band of the Q.P.D. stood close by, keeping an eye out.

Shortly after the paramedic arrived and placed Rebecca on a stretcher, her eyes fluttered open. Seeing him there, she mumbled, "Mark, what happened?"

"It's okay, you're safe now. You're gonna be fine, Becky. You were shot, but it only grazed you."

"Is everyone okay?"

"Don't worry about that for now, just let these men take care of you. I'm gonna have officer Clark stay with you, I have to finish here. Just rest for now."

"Be careful, Mark," she exclaimed, in a concerned tone of voice.

Moving away from him, the paramedics led her to the nearest ambulance, with Clark in tow. Looking at Kiara, he said, "I need you to go with your parents and those officers. They have to get you away from here."

"No, I want to stay with you. I'm scared," she cried.

"I know you are, honey, but you aren't safe in the open. You need to go, and I have to finish this. The killer may still be in the courthouse, and I can't take the risk of him trying to get you again. Please go, I'll come by the house as soon as I'm done here."

"Okay, Mr. St. James, but please be careful—and thank you for saving my life."

Watching her leave, he admired her courage. Even through her fear, and after all she'd been through, she cared what happened to him. Turning he went toward the courthouse. He arrived at the front door just as Stintz and Jon were coming out, arguing as usual.

"Can't you two just let bygones be bygones? We're in the middle of the biggest murder investigation since The Hangman, guys. I swear if you two don't stop soon, I'll use my influence in town to get both of you suspended," he exclaimed angrily.

Startled, both of them stopped and looked at him. Now was clearly not the time to fuck with him, so they just nodded and shut up.

"Now, what's going on? Have they found him yet?" he asked.

Glaring at Jon, Stintz replies, "No, the entire first floor is almost cleared and no one suspicious has left. Luckily, we were already planning on this, so we were able to react quickly. We believe he's still in the building somewhere."

"Good, then let's go get the bastard."

3:15 p.m.

Standing in Judge Teddy Van Bout's courtroom, he watched as the scene of the crime was processed. The bastard had done it again. Not only had he tricked them, but evidently, he'd planned all of these things days ago.

Lying on the floor in the front of the judge's bench was an unknown female victim, splayed out and cut open like a fish filleted at a Chinese restaurant. Apparently, this time The Surgeon was reenacting a kidney transplant. Eyes wide in fear, the woman had been clearly alive during the procedure again. Her nude body showed no visible signs of a struggle. The massive blood puddle surrounding the body indicated the type of death she had suffered.

Sitting in chairs at the prosecutors' and defendants' tables were four men. Their throats had been cut ear to ear. The M.E.'s assistants had already verified the victims' tongues were missing. Two of these victims had been identified. One was Todd Ratlein, who worked at the court house as a property clerk, and the other was Sid Bushman, the janitor. All clothing and property of the victims had been removed from the scene.

A separate set of investigators were by the window that looked down at the lawn. They were carefully dismantling a stand which held a laser sight. The killer had never been in this building at the time of the lawn shooting. He definitely was smart and resourceful. He had built a robotic, laser-sight, stand which he could control from a distance. To the best of their knowledge the receiver could get signals from up to a mile away.

The other buildings in the area were being searched, but it was already obvious The Surgeon was long gone. Mark was seething with frustration. He wanted to hit something. Once again, the man had killed and gotten away with it right under their noses.

Standing beside him, Jon asked, "Any word on Rebecca?"

"Yeah, she'll be fine. She's gonna have a scar, but other than that she should be able to go back to work tomorrow. That is, if she wants, and you know as well as I do, she will."

"I'm just glad she's okay. I guess her reaction to you, and the guy who went down beside her, was the only thing that saved her life. She's a lucky woman. Do we know why he did this yet?"

"If I didn't know better, I'd say he's just a fucked-up man getting his rocks off, but today tells me he's also playing with us."

"Why do you say that?"

"Because, obviously he wanted me to see the laser sight on Kiara and assume she was being targeted. He was watching us, Jon. As soon as I made my move, people started dying. He was waiting. He wants us to jump. This is all some kind of game. I just can't figure out what his end game is."

"So, where do we go from here?"

"Research, Jon, research. I'm gonna go find Soluchu and have a talk with him. We need to find out who The Surgeon is and what he wants before he strikes again."

Turning away, Mark walked out of the courtroom.

Chapter 15

Inquiries and Inquisitions

Wednesday, May 17
6:02 p.m.

Entering the Q.P.D., he approached the front desk and visited with the officer on duty. After working through the pleasantries, he finally got down to business and asked him, "Have you seen Soluchu around?"

"I know he was here earlier, might a went home already though. Want me to check his desk?"

"Could ya?"

"Will do, wait just a minute."

Turning around and looking out the entrance, he waited for the officer to finish checking on Soluchu for him. It was dusk outside, the moment between day and twilight. A beautiful sunset could be seen on the horizon, which was awash with purples, oranges and reds.

Standing here waiting for the officer, he found himself listing all the things he knew about The Surgeon. He was smart, ex-military, knew how to use scalpels and probably all of a surgeon's tools, knew how to handle weapons including sniper rifles, enjoyed slicing and dicing women, and always cleaned up afterwards. He appeared to be making a statement by the almost ritualistic way he killed. So far, all the events attributed to him had a female victim displayed in front of half a dozen to two dozen assorted victims. The word malignant was always at the scene. It's possible some of the sniper killings were his, but he was inclined to believe the killings today were more about Kiara than his M.O. Mark believed The Surgeon also either knew him, or had heard about him and wanted a challenge. That last was conjecture on his part, but it felt right.

Hearing the telephone being placed back on the receiver, he turned back to the man at the desk. Looking at the officer's face, he already knew he was in luck, so when he said, "Go on up, you just caught him," he was already in the motion of moving toward the door leading further into the station.

The Q.P.D. was located in a large two-story building at the corner of Broadway and Second. It resembled an old colonial style home, with brocaded eaves and slate roof tiles. The color on the outside wasn't much better than the inside. Half of the building was dedicated to the Police Department, the other had been slightly remodeled and currently housed the town's meager Fire Department.

Besides the Police Department's front desk, the first floor housed mostly interview rooms and most of the fire division, so Mark headed to the stairs near the rear of the building and took them two at a time.

Not knowing exactly where Soluchu was, he stopped at the nearest occupied desk and asked for directions. Apparently, he had been given an office, and was now a detective for the domestic crimes division. The second floor was divided up between police and fire again, but while downstairs was mostly fire, upstairs was mostly police. The center of the room contained the 911 operators' desk, which presently had three in attendance. Working the way out from there were desks for all the other current officers—at this hour, many of them were unoccupied due to the late hours. To the right were offices, mainly for the heads of various divisions, and at the back was the chief's office. Despite the clutter, the Q.P.D. was a well-oiled machine.

Walking down the corridor to Soluchu's office, he acknowledged several acquaintances, and said hi to friends from days when he was on the force. Stopping at the third door down, he knocked and waited for a response before walking in. Soluchu's office reflected the man's tastes. Coming from Spanish ancestry, he liked browns and blacks, which were the dominant colors in the room. Photos and art on the back wall reflected his appreciation of his heritage and family, while his certificates took up a portion of the wall on the left. In the center of the room was a desk with two chairs in front of it. Seated behind the desk was Frank Soluchu, himself.

Frank got up, walked around the desk, and gave Mark's hand a firm shake. Standing at five eleven, with long, wavy black hair and a dark bronze skin tone, it was plain why women seemed to chase after this man. Rumors had always been raging about Frank, but anyone who knew him well knew him to be a loyal husband and devoted father. It still surprised Mark how much he had grown up; he'd known him to be a very mischievous recruit while he had worked here.

"It's been a long time, Mark. We miss you up here."

"Yeah, it's good to see you again too, Frank."

"I'm glad to see you survived everything. I'm still really sorry how it all went down. Oh, and I'm even more sorry to hear about the present circumstances."

"Don't worry about it, and thanks for the concern. Hate to forgo all the pleasantries, and would love to catch up sometime, but I'm here on business."

"Thought you might be, have a seat and we'll talk."

Sitting down we got down to the point of the visit, "What do you remember about The Surgeon from your days in my squad?"

"Actually, not much, at least nothing you probably don't already know. You're in luck though, because I recently got online and did a search to refresh my memories. What do you want to know?"

"First of all, has the FBI done a psych profile on the killer, and what do we know about his personal life?"

And so, the rabbit began to chase the fox.

8:10 p.m.

As The Surgeon walked in the back door, Chicanery said, "Heard about the show. Excellently done, but why didn't you kill the girl?"

"Because I want to have fun with him, and toying with his pride is just the beginning. The girl will die, that you can be sure of."

"And why hasn't the second job been done yet? You told me days ago you were almost ready. I hope this game you're playing with St. James hasn't spoiled my plans."

"It will be done, I just wanted to put a hold on my time line, because I heard there's a better opportunity coming up. One which will draw more victims to the table. You sound as if you doubt me."

"No, it's not that, but I've made inquiries of my own. It seems you have less of a hold on your game with St. James than you think. He's been asking questions, and making appearances at places that could put you at risk. I've decided to advance my time line on a future plan."

"Oh yeah? And what's that?" The Surgeon inquired.

"Your show today was indeed excellent, but it also helped me start round two of my plans, if a bit sooner than I intended. I've called in a friend, who will hopefully help further confuse the police in this town. You will be working with him from now on."

Outraged, he responded, "I don't work with anyone. I can do this on my own. How dare you do this without consulting me?"

"Once again you try my patience. I am your employer. I pay you to act, not talk. You will do as I say or else. Now get the fuck out of my sight."

With a look of utter hatred in his eyes, The Surgeon stormed out of the house.

Chapter 16

The Show Must Go On

Friday, May 19
6:36 p.m.

Alex "Sureshot" Sheridan leisurely pedaled the bike up a small hill on the bike trail. He wasn't a big man, but he wouldn't be considered small either. He was of average height, and weighed about 190. Most people would have considered him overweight, if they didn't notice his bulging arm and leg muscles. While most runners and weight lifters like to display the results of their efforts, he preferred anonymity.

Sureshot turned a corner in the trail, and noticed a healthy, perspiring red head coming his way. The athletic bra and shirt the woman was wearing helped to emphasize her ample tits. Very nice. He briefly allowed himself a moment to imagine them bouncing in front of his face as she'd ride him, the same way they did as she rode her bike, then she was past him.

Sureshot was a name other kids had given him growing up, because no matter the activity, football or baseball all the way down to darts, he was always right on target. He was always the first chosen for teams. After a while his friends began conning new-bies in town. They made bets, and at first, he acted like he might lose—but then he earned everything, plus some extra, back. It wasn't until the accidental death of one of his marks that he had stopped.

Although no one knew it, that death had been the defining moment of his life. From that day forward he became obsessed with death. As of the age of 16, Sureshot had felt the need to become familiar with it and all its forms. Even now, almost thirty years later, he could remember how it felt to not only crush that man's nose, but to watch him die as the splinters flew into his brain. Even in that he was a Sureshot. Pulling off to the side of the trail, he climbed off, then grabbed the picnic basket out of the bike rack on back and walked off a distance into the sparse trees. Setting the basket down, pulling out a large blanket, and laying it out on the ground, he used a few rocks to weigh down the corners. Spreading out all the food, drinks and miscellaneous supplies on the left side of the blanket, he walked back to his bike. Moving it back into the foliage, he leaned it up against some mulberry bushes. Sitting down to wait, he grabbed a double bo-logna, double salami, ham and cheese sandwich out of a Tupper-ware container and took a bite.

7:32 p.m.

From a distant hill behind the Quincy Drive-In, The Surgeon watched as cars pulled up, paid for their tickets and found spots for the show. This evening's movie was a thriller about a babysit-ter, harassed by frequent phone calls from a stranger who even-tually tried to kill her. It was supposed to start at eight o'clock sharp.

The Surgeon aimed his binoculars at the small playground that sets in a small field in front of the theaters' projector screen. The easy part had already been done, for he had already loosened several boards in the fence surrounding the drive-in on two sides. Now all he had to do was wait. He'd chosen this night not only for the estimated regular attendance, but because the movie was said to be set mostly at night and would provide plenty of darkness.

Looking at his watch, he began to feel the electricity and heat that always rose in his body before he killed. Sometimes he couldn't tell which is more exciting: the kill or the way he felt before. He could feel his erect cock throbbing and pulsating in his black jeans as if it too was anticipating what would happen next. He never masturbated at times like this. It would only violate his first rule: duty overcame pleasure.

Glancing at his watch again, he began putting his supplies back into the pouches connected to his belt.

8:10 p.m.

Sureshot glanced at his watch, stood up and pulled the bottom out of the picnic basket. Underneath, he found the parts to his PSG1 Sniper Rifle. He quickly assembled it, lay on the ground, then began setting up the bi-pod attached to the bottom of the rifle. Looking through the scope, he watched as the movie's opening credits began. Apparently, the commercials at the beginning had just ended.

Grabbing another sandwich, he took a bite, aimed through the scope, adjusted, and pulled the trigger. A slight buck hit his shoulder, and he watched as a head exploded, displaying a cloud of red mist. He immediately pulled the trigger again, and the second person's head in the car exploded before they could react. In quick succession, six more people died.

8:22 p.m.

Slipping through the fence after removing the slats, he entered the theater area. Silently weaving throughout the cars, The Surgeon picked his targets, made contact, and moved on quickly. In less than five minutes he'd chosen his victims, and he had yet to be noticed. Making his way back to the first target, he stopped when he saw what appears to be brain matter on the ground beside a car door. Checking it out, he realizes Chicanery's friend must have shown up already. This knowledge made The Surgeon's blood boil, yet at the same time he was fascinated by the death in front of him. It gave him pause as he admires the two victims in the car.

Moving on, it dawned on him that he needed to hurry in case this other man accidentally hit him or killed one of his victims. Quickly lifting each victim and placing them onto his shoulders in a fireman's carry, he took them to the playground area. One of the most arousing parts of killing was how he could feel the slightest heartbeat and intake of breath while carrying them. In less than fifteen minutes he was laying the final victim on the merry-go-round. Standing up, he watched her eyes widen as he began to remove her clothing. Little by little, her breathe quickened as he carefully took all of her clothes off and folded them up, placing them neatly on the ground.

After the woman was completely naked, The Surgeon moves to the fence line and begins hauling cheap beach chairs to the site, setting them up in a circle around the merry-go-round. He then began lifting each of the eighteen other victims he'd chosen onto the chairs and arranging their bodies so they would appear to be watching, after which he moved toward the woman. The Surgeon observed the eyes of the bystanders as he pulled the scalpel from a pouch on his belt. He smiled as all their pupils appeared to widen involuntarily when he made the first incision into the woman's chest.

8:36 p.m.

Scanning the theater parking lot through the scope, Sureshot saw a black man weaving in and out among the cars. He watched as the man known to him as The Surgeon paused near a car door of someone he had just dispatched. He appeared to be admiring the handiwork. Focusing in on The Surgeon's face he memorized its features for future use, then watched as his face contorted from expressions of anger to arousal.

Returning to his job, he pulled the trigger three times in quick succession, then took another bite of his sandwich.

8:59 p.m.

The Surgeon finished deftly writing the word malignant above the woman's head with her own blood. Standing up, he appraised the scene, gave a nod of approval, then turned toward his audience. He could see the terror in each of the various individuals' eyes. Their panic had set in; unfortunately, he noticed a few who had passed out and one who may have died already from a stroke or heart attack, given the vacant look in his eyes.

Walking toward the nearest member of the audience, a young man of about twenty, The Surgeon gripped his face along the jawline, grabbed the tongue with a set of pliers removed from a pouch in his belt, and sliced it neatly off with the razor-sharp scalpel. Placing it in a baggie he stepped behind the boy, pulled his head back and cut his throat with one brief stroke of the scalpel.

Moving on, he repeated the process on the remaining seventeen, including the one already dead.

8:55 p.m.

Glancing briefly through his scope at The Surgeon's progress, Sureshot watched as he put the finishing touches on woman's body on the merry-go-round. The precision of his work was mesmerizing, almost paralyzingly so. Forcing himself to pull his eyes away from the sight, just as the boy's throat was cut, he finished the sandwich and began cleaning up the site.

CHAPTER 17

CREDITS

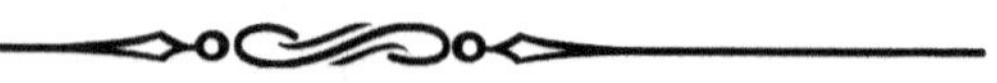

Friday, May 19
9:35 p.m.

As the credits begin to roll, the lights came on and cars started up. Gus Lichtman, the Drive-In's owner, watched some of the youth begin whooping and hollering, while some parents allowed their children to head toward the playground for a few last minutes of fun. He has always enjoyed owning this theater. His father had built it in 1966, when he was 42 years old. Gus remembered watching his father, and other workers, building everything when he was ten.

When his father died of a heart attack at the age of 73, he had been working here. Gus had had to work hard to get permission from the studios to have In memory of Buddy Lichtman placed at the end of all the movies. The memorial was for the drive-in itself, not the movie.

Forty years later, the theater still made its profits, but it was the general population's enjoyment which kept Gus going. The smiles and laughter after each viewing were the heart and soul of things to him. So, when he suddenly heard loud screams and cries of anguish from the direction of the playground, as well as from multiple areas of the parking lot, he felt his first moments of fear.

Running toward the nearest commotion, and yelling at the some of the other attendants to see what was going on, Gus skidded to a top in front of the most horrifying sight of his entire life. Hanging partially out of the car window was a woman's head, it was missing part of its left side. Brain matter and coagulating blood pooled on the ground. Immediately, he found himself involuntarily puking the contents of his stomach.

Regaining control of his faculties, he pulled his cell phone out of his pocket and dialed 911.

10:36 p.m.

Mark had been on his way home from the Bensons' when he'd gotten the call from Kidd. When he looked at the caller I.D., he had a feeling he was going to dread the conversation. Answering the cell all he heard was, "Get to the Drive-In ASAP," then a click. If he hadn't recognized the rushed sound of Kidd's voice, he'd have never followed through, and would have reacted a lot differently. As it was, he went, suspecting the worst.

Pulling onto the street where the Drive In resided, he witnessed a display of chaos and panic. Up and down the street pedestrians wandered and stood watching as police tried to keep the peace at a blockade set up at the two entrances to the theater. There were two news vans from outside of Quincy as well as the local news at the scene with their cameras rolling and lights flashing. That brought forth memories of another time and place. He had always found the media to be insensitive and callous, but ever since that night several years ago he'd totally despised them.

Driving up to the blockade, he displayed his I.D. and was waved through by a sergeant. Turning his car away from what appeared to be the crime scene, he parked near the rest of the cop cars in the area. Stepping out of the vehicle he was assaulted by the overwhelming smell of death in the air, the sound of yelling and crying, and the powerful theater lights used to dispel the darkness.

Looking around, he spotted Kidd talking to some other officer near the snack stand. The Snack Shack was about the size of an elongated pavilion, and as the name implied was the drive in's store. Walking over to Kidd, he stopped a short distance away and waited till he could get her attention.

A few minutes later, she noticed him standing there and waved him over. Walking up to the small crowd of officers, several of which he knew by sight, if not by name, he asked, "So, what's the situation?"

"We've got a hell of a mess, that's the situation. How the media, especially out of the area ones, found out this quickly I'll never figure out. This was just called in about 45 minutes ago," Kidd responded in frustration.

"You know how I feel about the media ever since my family was killed, so I know you didn't call me in for them. What can I do about the mess? What's the status on things here? How many dead this time?"

"Sorry, Mark, just blowing off some steam. It looks like The Surgeon really had fun tonight. At last count twenty minutes ago, we have 73 dead. A lot of men and women, some teens and two children. It's a damn shame what happened tonight."

"Yeah, sounds like another bad one," he empathized.

"It gets worse. Mark, I hate to tell you this, but two kids were hung, the same as the woman at the restaurant!"

"God damn it! When will this nightmare end," he exclaimed angrily.

"I'm really sorry, Mark. I'd advise against checking it out till they've been taken down. They weren't actually found until a while after we got here. We think either The Surgeon wanted them found later or someone else is doing it."

"Where were they found?" he asked, his voice tight from the struggle to control himself.

"Don't worry about that for now. It won't do you any good to run in and have a breakdown on us."

"Why does everyone think they know what's best for me? I can handle this myself, trust me. I know what the fuck I'm doing and what I can handle! Now, where?"

Startled and slightly perturbed by his demeanor and stature, Kidd took a step back, then stated, "In the women's room."

He had turned toward the restroom and started in that direction, when he felt a restraining hand on his arm. Looking back, he saw Jon standing there with a determined facial expression. Speaking sternly, he said, "You're not going in there, Mark. Not by yourself, and not in this state of mind."

"The hell I'm not Jon! I have to see, I gotta know what happened and why."

"Fine, but I'm going with you," he said in a tone that brooked no argument.

Knowing he was on the edge, Mark took a few deep breaths and headed toward the restroom again with Jon and Kidd following. Pushing open the door, he found the C.S.U. team hard at work and at the same time realized that all three of them weren't going to be able to fit in the room with those already there. Pausing in the doorway, he covered his mouth as the foul stench of death wafted from the room. As he glanced at Kidd, she nodded and told the crew, "Make some room--a few of you clear out. I need the room for a minute." Everyone except the two photographers, stepped out and Mark walked further into the room.

The scene was sickening, and if he hadn't seen one similar in the past, he probably would have lost his supper. Hanging silently from two of the stall frames were two children. They couldn't have been younger than two, or older than six. Both had contusions and cuts on their hands, arms, legs and face – just like the restaurant owner. The most dominant thing he noticed was that their stomachs had been laid open and their intestines strung around their bodies, then up to the top frame and then back down around their throats. As they swung lifelessly, blood pooled on the floor under them in a large oval, connected by an almost bridge-like trail of coagulated blood.

Tears streaming down his face, Mark stormed out of the restroom with a hatred close to madness for The Surgeon.

✦ 96 ✦

CHAPTER 18

DEATH AND A MOVIE

Friday, May 19
10:58 p.m.

Rushing out the door of the restroom, Mark knocked down a technician standing just outside the door. Seething with anger, he barely noticed. Jon gave the man a hand up, brushed him off, and apologized for Mark. Catching up to Kidd and Mark, he heard Kidd saying: "...calm down. I can't have you acting up like this. You're gonna hurt someone or yourself."

"I'm fine, Kidd. In fact, my head has never been clearer on anything in my life. Whoever is killing these people wanted to shame and destroy me, but all he did was open a door inside that I shut when I left Iraq," Mark's body was clearly trembling—and then suddenly it was not, as if a switch had been flipped. Jon watched this transformation come over his friend and felt an icy chill run along his spine. In appearances it was like a storm had just cleared, but in reality, he knew Mark was riding in the eye of it. He remained silent, knowing that the killer had invoked a force in Mark that he did not want to come in contact with.

Kidd had obviously noticed the change in Mark's body as well, because she suddenly began talking a lot less firmly and a lot more quietly, "Listen, I know this is a bad situation, and I'm sorry we're here again. I need your head clear on this one. I can't afford another dead killer. Now I know it wasn't your fault, I'd have done the same thing if I'd have found my family that way, but we need to go by the book. I can't afford another internal investigation, Mark."

"I told you I'm fine. I won't kill him, but I will catch him one way or another."

Still walking close behind the other two, they finally made their way across the parking lot, where the vehicles that weren't needed had already been cleared away. Now there were only four cars, two trucks and a van left. The automobiles which belonged to the victims in the playground area had been tagged and moved to a cordoned off area down the road a bit. Those remaining in the area held the gunshot victims and were being cleared by the C.S.U. crew.

Approaching the crew near the victims in the playground he watched as Mark strolled up, clearly in control, and began observing the scene. He saw him watching the medical examiner, the most. It was clear he cared for her, though as for how far that went, Jon had no idea. Stepping up to Mark, he finally broke the silence, "So, what do you think?"

Glancing over, Mark's eyes were cold and calculating, and after a brief moment he said, "I think this is a very sick man, and when I catch him, he won't like what happens. I told her I wouldn't kill him; I didn't say how I'd bring him in."

"I heard all that, I just want to know if you have any thoughts about the scene in front of us."

"My thoughts, you want to know my thoughts? It's simple, the guy's a sick fuck who needs his limbs torn off his body. That's what I think. But from a professional standpoint, I'd say someone he was close to had cancer and died for whatever reason. The tongue's removal and slit throats could be either because the killer wasn't told about it or he was lied to about how it happened. The fact that the main victim of an apparent 'operation' is always female indicates the person that he was close to was probably a significant other or mother. That's what I think about the situation in front of us as well as the last one and all the deaths recorded on the net," Mark replied soberly.

"I think you probably got pretty close to the truth with those observations."

Standing observing the scene before him, he waited for things to settle down. He didn't like seeing Mark so shut down and cold; he'd been his friend for years, and even his partner. This was the first time he'd ever seen him like this. After the death of his family, he'd witnessed Mark become depressed, desolated, angry and distraught, but never emotionless. He thought he'd seen him through all of his ups and downs, but apparently, he had not. This was a side Jon never had known was there. If he hadn't known Mark, he would have been scared. He was just glad he didn't have to face Mark's wrath.

Rebecca came up and joined them, interrupting his thoughts, and said, "Another mock surgery done before a silent audience. This time it was supposed to be a heart transplant. The heart was placed in a jar with the same fluid as before, and placed beside the victim's clothes. Luckily, I didn't recognize the victim, but found the I.D. in her purse and her name was Pyta Lazgood."

"The name is unfamiliar to me as well. A welcome relief, after what I saw inside the restroom," he said without emotion.

Looking at Mark, an expression of concern came across Rebecca's features and she said, "I'm sorry you saw that. Are you okay? You sound, ah, different."

"I'm fine."

Taken aback at his tone, she glanced quickly at Jon—but then looked backed toward Mark and said, "Well, okay then, if you need me later you know where I am. Just don't lose sight of your friends, Mark."

"Thanks. What else can you tell me about this? We need to find The Surgeon before he kills again."

"To the best of our knowledge there weren't any witnesses this time, at least no one's stepped forward. We don't know everyone who was here, obviously, but in the only statement we've made to the media so far, we asked anyone with knowledge of what happened here to come forward. It should have already gone out on the 10:30 news.

We believe he used the cover of darkness to select his victims and kill them, especially in light of the kind of movie which was playing. There's a board missing from the fence to the left of the projection screen, and seems to be the point of entry. There weren't any prints anywhere. He was just as professional as the last time. I'm not surprised that no one knows who this guy is. One of the victims was about 225 pounds, which supports my earlier conclusion that the killer is male. And finally, the gunshot victims indicate that there may be two killers here; either that, or he was extremely quick.

The gunshot victims appear to have the same wounds as the ones at the memorial service. That makes it seem as though The Surgeon is the sole killer, or at least he wants us to believe so. I'll be able to make a better assessment when the ballistics have been completed.

I have to admit our killer hasn't made any mistakes which would give us a clue to his identity yet, but I'll keep digging. I can't really give you much to help in finding him, Mark. I'm sorry."

"Just let me know if you find out anything more. I guess I'll just have to find a clue to The Surgeon's identity by looking deeper into his past. I'll find him, though."

Again that look of concern passed over her features, but this time she remained silent. Watching this interaction between them was painful for Jon. It was almost as if Mark had turned and shut the door on all the good things in his world, so that he could face the evil ones without allowing them to affect him.

"You know how to reach me when you learn something more," Mark said, and then turned, strolling away apparently consumed by his own thoughts.

Chapter 19

Shaky Alliances

Saturday, May 20
9:06 a.m.

Strolling down the streets of Quincy, The Surgeon could see the fear and mistrust festering among the residents. When he'd first arrived in town, he'd seen kids running or riding a bike up and down neighborhood streets, adults had been talking animatedly, and teenagers could be seen holding hands with their lovers or up to some sort of mischief. Now, just a mere three weeks after he'd begun his missions, everyone was more cautious and reserved.

It was a Saturday morning and the Quincy Public Park looked deserted and abandoned. It could be that people were still shocked by the massacre at the drive-in, just two streets away, or maybe it was that no one wanted to lose their own life as others had. Either way, it was of no concern to him. He was here only to complete the assignments, and then kill St. James. The only things that mattered in this town were the mission and his personal vendetta.

Still, it was interesting how people reacted to death. Each person seemed to react differently: one was in grief, another was shocked, some were completely indifferent - or maybe just unaware - and then there seemed to be a few who were intrigued by the idea. Those were the exception. For the most part, the reaction was outrage. Outrage that it could happen in their town. Outrage that it could happen to someone they knew. And just simply outrage that it could happen. To the last one he smiled.

Continuing down First, The Surgeon mused over the newest killer Chicanery had brought in, supposedly to decrease the heat he was bringing down upon himself. Sureshot was a man he could admire, although working with someone else wasn't his style. He especially didn't like working with someone who didn't see the mission and play by the rules. Things were getting a bit complicated, but in all of the chaos he knew St. James would pay. Sureshot was a killer for hire, pure and simple. He hadn't met the man yet, but from what he'd seen at the drive-in, the man was good. From what Chicanery had told him about Sureshot, he appeared to be a psychopath. The Surgeon knew a lot about psychopaths. As a general rule, he found it very displeasing to work with them, but it appeared he didn't have a choice this time. He just hoped he could leave this town and this entire mission behind soon.

Cutting across the Quincy Public Park, he made his way back toward the safe house. Walking under oak, beech, birch, maple, elm and walnut trees and around the pine trees, he found the walk relaxing and exhilarating. It was refreshing his mind and clearing his emotions about the situation at hand. Walking up a low hill, he reached the crest to find a bunch of teenage boys and girls on the basketball court.

On a whim, he chose to enjoy the cleansing atmosphere and grabbed a seat on one of the benches. Watching the clumsy boys playing ball and trying to impress the girls was humorous and brought back memories. The innocence of these teenagers disgusted him. The Surgeon did not miss those days in his life, because he now knew how vulnerable and gullible innocence had made him. Even through the disgust he could find humor, although it was a twisted kind.

He considered how easily his Navy training would have made it for him to quickly dispatch all the kids on the court. His blood began to boil and his heart beat faster as he envisioned each individual's death. Everything slowed in his mind, and he could feel the hardness of his cock against his leg as he imagined each and every person on the court and in the bleachers, their bones broken and their bodies bleeding out.

A smile broke out on his face, he blinked, and the game progressed. Teenage girls squealed with pleasure or yelled encouragement to their men. Others shyly watched boys they liked, though they couldn't manage to let their attraction be known. The Surgeon found passiveness and a lack of assertion funny as well. Again, these were traits of the weak, a word he'd never again allow to describe himself.

Getting up, he moved leisurely toward Second and stopped in front of Chicanery's home. Swallowing his dislike for this house, his point of safety in this town, he walked up to the gate, went into the backyard, then entered the home through the back door as usual. Trying to avoid further confrontation he headed to the basement stairs. All was quiet.

Opening the door to the cache, he stopped when he saw Chicanery sitting on the bed and another man in the La-Z- Boy. The man appeared to be about five and a half feet tall, athletically built, and intelligent. He had black, slicked-back hair, grey eyes, and a long, slightly bent nose. His light skin tone was almost translucent, and he had a mole below his right ear.

"Hello Kyle, meet Alex. He was your support during the mission last night. I wanted you to meet him before I give you the specs for your next and final mission. I've made sure all is in place for you to receive your chance to do maximum damage, tie up loose ends, and kill St. James," Chicanery declared.

With a sigh and a roll of his eyes, The Surgeon walked into the room and leaned up against the south wall. He nodded at the man named Alex, and glanced at Chicanery before replying,

"I'm growing weary of these missions. There is more and more risk of my getting caught, and I want St. James now. The longer I wait, the more chance I won't get to kill him. You've already told me he's closing in on me. At least that was why you told me he," nodding toward Alex, "was brought in."

Sighing in frustration, Chicanery answered through gritted teeth, "I've already paid you $750,000 for the first two missions. Since this mission involves slightly more risk than the last two, I'll pay you this combined amount as a bonus. Now can we get down to business?"

"Sure. What's the target?"

Chicanery picked up a manila envelope which was laying on the bed beside him. Handing the envelope to The Surgeon, he began talking . . .

1:52 p.m.

Walking into his office, Mark sat down on his Ethan Allen black leather couch. Stretching, rubbing his eyes, and yawning, he tried to relax. These last three weeks were bringing a tension into his body that he hadn't felt since his time as the head of S.C.I.U.

Looking around his office, he reflected on how he'd come about obtaining this space. The room was larger than most, at 100 square feet. Descending from the town's founder had earned him a lot of headaches in the past, but it also meant having more money than he needed. He'd enjoyed the life's comforts he could afford, and therefore had a well-decorated office.

On the walls hung several expensive pictures, tapestries and certificates that documented his many achievements. Many of the pictures were reprints of Thomas Kinkade classics. However, there were also the Rembrandts and Van Gogh's. His favorite, and most relaxing, picture was the large Kinkade hanging above his fireplace. The fireplace was stone, it was made of blue and grey granite and covered the middle-bottom half of the wall opposite his couch. To the left and right of the fireplace were photo frames of his dead wife and children. It was a collage of memorabilia to commemorate his family.

In the center of the room was a gold inlaid, redwood desk. There was a black leather office chair behind it, and two black leather cushioned chairs in front of the desk. On the right corner of the desk sat a crystal touch lamp. In the middle of the room was a large Aztec floor rug.

When he'd first bought the building in which his office currently resided, it had cost $75,000. At first, he had rented the office across the hall to an insurance salesman, but his business became well known so he had moved up in the world. Now the building seemed lonely at times. He'd chosen this building for two reasons: it provided a good view of the high school football and softball fields, two of his favorite sports, and it was close to the courthouse.

At present, the office across the hall wasn't rented. It doubled as his P.T. room and a place to crash when he didn't want to go home from the job. Since the exhaustion he felt was mental, he knew it wouldn't do him any good to make use of it. His mind still churned with theories of whom The Surgeon could be, and what was coming next. So far, there hadn't been any more attacks on Kiara, and no indication of an impending one. All of the attacks had happened within a week or so of each other. They had been extremely public and had left from one to three dozen victims in their wake.

He expected another attack soon. Mark believed he was running out of time to stop The Surgeon. He knew more were going to die. The Surgeon had been doing this for years, in ten different countries, and the knowledge they had of him was minimal at best. Mark wasn't looking forward to the idea that was gelling in his mind, but he didn't think there was another choice. Kidd's suggestion after the drive-in incident was valid. They needed the town to be safe, and they needed to minimize The Surgeon's activities and the casualty rate. Picking up his phone, he pressed a speed dial number. Kidd answered on the third ring, "Yes, Mark, what's up?"

"I don't like it, but you may be right. We need help on this one. Call FBI, and tell them what's going on."

"Are you sure? You know what happened when they were called in on The Hangman case."

"I think we're out of options here. However, I think we should make use of the media. Inform them about the FBI being called in, and talk about the extra security measures we want to take to ensure the town's safety."

"I was gonna have to do this anyway, but I'm glad you're on board, Mark."

"I don't really have a choice, do I?" He hung up.

Chapter 20

Kiara's Invitation

Sunday, May 21
11:12 a.m.

I really don't know how much longer I'll be unable to come to school. Everything is a bit scary right now. I mean my boyfriend died, and then someone tried to kill me at the memorial. I hope to attend our annual exhibition football game, but I still need to convince my parents, Kiara typed.

We all miss you. Cliff says his mom wants to see you at his birthday party next Saturday, but she understands if you can't make it. I think it's Cliff that really wants you to be there. You know how jealous he always acted around Daniel. Popped up on her screen.

Kiara didn't like being stuck at home almost all the time, but she understood the reasons. The attack on Daniel's and the rest of the victims' memorial had her shaken up, even now, four days later. She was thankful to be alive, though even that felt like it was a betrayal of Daniel. She just hoped she could remain alive and do something to honor his name.

She was also glad for the Internet. She'd been able to keep up with school, and stay in communication with her friends. Without her computer, being in home protection would have been unbearable.

Yes, I know. He was really annoying when he was around us. I'll try to be there, though, because he is a good friend nevertheless. Let's hope by then I won't need protection anymore.

Waiting for the response, Kiara considered what she would say to her parents to convince them to allow her to attend the football game. Obviously - with all the heightened security precautions in town - the game would be well protected. She would promise to never leave the side of the officers or Mark. In addition, she'd argue everyone needed time away from the house. All in all, she thought her chances were good.

We can hope. If you can make it to the game on Thursday, meet me in the girls' locker room for some girl time. I know your parents, and some cops, can't be the best company in the world, especially with the loss of Daniel. Carmaine was always so thoughtful. She could definitely use some down time with her friends, and it shouldn't be a problem going into the locker room.

If I can convince my parents, I'll be there.

Kiara considered all the times it had been Daniel on the other end of the network. All the many long nights she had stayed up communicating via the Net. All the times he'd snuck into her bedroom without her parents' knowledge. The many times they'd cuddled in bed and playfully fondled each other.

Tears began to roll down Kiara's face. The screen blurred in front of her. Her friend had responded, but she couldn't get herself to do so. Placing her face in her hands, she began to sob loudly.

A quiet knock, and she heard her mom's delicate voice saying, "Are you okay honey? Can I come in?"

Unable to respond immediately, she continued to sob, then replied, "I'm fine, Mom. Just thinking about Daniel again."

"Do you want me to get anything for you?"

"No, I'll be okay."

Grabbing some tissue, she blew her nose, blinked her eyes to clear her vision, and started typing: *Sorry, slow in responding, emo-*

tions are still on a hair trigger. I'll talk to my mom and see if she can get the cops to let you spend the night. Just don't invite too many others. Stacey, Katherine, and Kimmy should be okay.

Let me know. I'll keep it to a minimum.

Backing out of the Palsmessenger Chatline, she walked out of her bedroom, across the hall, and into the bathroom. Splashing water on her face, she took a few deep breaths and examined herself in the mirror. Fortunately, she didn't have a reason to put makeup on, otherwise here face would have had smears running down it. She missed Daniel more than she could express in words.

Leaving the bathroom, she walked down the hall and took a right into the kitchen. Her mother was standing at the counter putting mayo on some whole wheat bread. There was a spread of lettuce, tomatoes, onions, pickles, and various lunch meats on the counter in front of her. Always the faithful housewife and mother, she was preparing lunch.

Plopping down in a chair at the table, she asked her mother, "Whacha making?"

"Thought we'd have sandwiches and chips for lunch out back. I figured we've been cooped up long enough. A semi-picnic would be good for us all."

"Sounds good, mom. Speaking of being cooped up, some of my friends wanted to come over tonight for a sleep over. Tomorrow is Memorial Day, so I figured it would be good for us."

"I don't see a problem with it. We'll need to run it by the officers and dad, but it shouldn't be a big deal. Besides, you deserve something like that."

"Thanks mom. I'll let them know. Also, graduation is on Wednesday, followed by the school's annual exhibition football game on Thursday. Since security will be tight - with everything that's happened and all - I'd like to go."

Looking up at her daughter with concern in her eyes, she said, "We'll have to discuss it dear. Graduation is important, so we will definitely try to get you there. I don't know about the football game though. It's kinda risky."

"Oh, come on mom. The field will be surrounded by cops, and I'll have a personal escort."

"I'll think about it."

"Okay."

Getting up, Kiara headed toward her bedroom to let Carmaine know about the sleep over.

Chapter 21

Meetings

Monday, May 22 Memorial Day
8:22 a.m.

- Annapolis, Maryland –

Riding through downtown Annapolis, Mark admired all of the older structures. The brick, marble, granite, and stone houses spoke of true masonry craftsmanship. All around him were business and residential homes, only differing in style by size and color, but everyone had in common the simple things. Windows, doors, siding, porches, and roofing were designed in all manner of the most intricate and exquisite ways. Driving through this city was almost like passing through a section of history itself. It was simply extraordinary. On the horizon he could see the Atlantic Ocean go on for miles, as if the world were nothing but water on this side of the continent. Coming upon an old steel mill - still producing steel - produced an intense feeling of satisfaction. Being a native of Pennsylvania, he was used to seeing them frequently, but it was all a nice reminder of home.

He was here to meet with an old military friend. Since it was Memorial Day weekend, it afforded his friend an opportunity to get away from the Pentagon for a few days. Major Arthur T. Brusskin had been his recruiter when he'd first joined the Navy. Arthur had grown up in Baltimore, but kept a small cottage for leisure activities here. Ever since his wife had died when he was 53 years old, this had become his second home. He seldom spent time at his house in Baltimore anymore.

He had flown down to Baltimore from Pittsburgh yesterday evening, after calling Arthur to check on his plans for the weekend. Arthur told him it was just going to be himself and a few friends spending time on the Chesapeake Bay fishing and invited him down. Mark immediately hopped on a plane and took him up on his invitation. He hadn't slept in almost seventy-two hours, at least not effectively. He was working on his tenth cup of hot coffee in two hours. He knew he looked like shit.

Pulling into the harbor, he found Arthur's boat easily enough. It was a large charter boat customized for deep sea fishing, with all the amenities of a high end mini-yacht. As he climbed aboard, the captain set off; apparently the guys were anxious to be on their way. Walking down the galley stairs, he found the Major and three of his friends at the bar. Joining them, he ordered an orange-juice, and began listening to the tail end of their conversation about the Middle East.

Arthur introduced Alexander, Greg, and Jimmy as their companions for the trip. Alex was a family friend, and the other two worked at the office with him. Taking into consideration why he might be here, the Major included that they were all trustworthy. As always, the Major was nothing if he wasn't thorough.

There was a platter of sausage, bacon, ham, and potatoes cooked in various manners, along with various other main dishes and muffins. Mark dug in - starved as he was - and ate a good portion of everything in between cups of juice and coffee. As he ate, Arthur updated him on all the news at the Pentagon and the military.

It was midmorning when they finished breakfast and headed up to the deck. While Arthur and Mark went to sit under the canopy, his friends baited their hooks and began fishing. Not knowing really where to begin, he nursed his cup of coffee until the Major asked, "You've never been so quiet before, son. What's on your mind?"

"Have you heard anything about what's been going on up in Quincy lately, Arthur?"

"Well, rumor has it you've got a lot of deaths on your hands, and that the FBI has showed up on the scene."

"Nothing gets by you. Yeah, that's the case. I'm here to discuss The Surgeon with you."

"Why? What's his connection, and why are you involved?"

"I'm involved because somehow the recent deaths are connected to The Hangman I killed several years ago." He must have visibly cringed at the mention of The Hangman, because Arthur suddenly looked sympathetic. "And all of the evidence leads us to believe our killer is The Surgeon."

"What makes you think The Surgeon is connected to The Hangman? Also, why do you think The Hangman's connected? There's never been a rumor or news of that."

"It's one of the things we've managed to keep out of the news. So far, during each attack, one or more of the victims were killed in the same way as The Hangman's M.O. The killer seems to be taunting me directly. The first was a young woman, and the second were two children, a boy and girl. It seems as though this new killer studied The Hangman and he's gunning for me next." He paused long enough to take a breath and drink some coffee. Besides he could tell his anger was rising by the tone of his voice. Taking a deep breath, he continued, "Whoever it is - The Surgeon or just some other sadistic bastard - it's really straining me. I truly thought I was going to kill someone last Friday, after the last attack. The other thing we've kept from the media, because of the horrifying nature of the information, is that the killer is somehow using Latrodectus to paralyze his victims to keep them alive before he kills them. According to the FBI database all of the victims assumed to be killed by The Surgeon had the same venom in their system during the autopsy."

"I'm really sorry about the bad business being brought up about your family. In regards to The Surgeon all we know is rumor and hearsay. Nothing has been substantiated. There haven't been any witnesses that we know of, and for all intents and purposes, The Surgeon is an enigma. As you already said, the assumed victims did have Latrodectus in their system, but it's all assumption. We nicknamed him The Surgeon, because all of the victims we've attributed to him were killed in the manner of some sort of surgery. Whether it was organ transplants, bypasses, biopsies, appendectomies, or exploratory, all of the victims suffered death at the hands of this man in the likeness of these surgeries." Sitting back, taking a breath, and apparently contemplating what to discuss next, Arthur tapped a finger on his chin. A blank look came over his green eyes, and he appeared to visibly age as he considered what he would say next. Mark could see his light gray hair wave in the breeze and his nose wrinkle at the smell of salt in the air from the bay. Finally his eyes refocused, and he said, "The other common factors are: the killer always uses a woman for the surgery victim, there always seem to be at least two victims with their throats cut and tongues either missing or hanging from their throat, the main victim's death is always orchestrated to look like a malpractice victim, the word malignant is always written in blood at the scene, and all the victims seem to have been alive while the killer worked on them. Fortunately, in the last six years, since the first incident we've been lucky enough to keep the final two factors hush-hush."

"That is extremely lucky, but this time I believe the killer may have made his first mistakes. One, there is a witness this time, and two, from what I've read all the incidents in the past were isolated. We've had 2 in two weeks, and one attempt on the witness's life."

"How reliable is the witness?"

"Unfortunately, it was dark and the killer took the lights out; however, either our killer is black or he wore a mask. He also was quite tall because he didn't have a problem looking out the bathroom window. I would use the witness as bait, but I believe he's toying with me, like he thinks it's a game or something." He then began describing the attempt on Kiara's life to the Major. "So I think now is our best bet at catching the killer."

"You might be right. This is the first time he's ever stayed in one place so long. And from what you've described, I would try and find a connection to someone in your past. Although I do think the connection with The Hangman is just the killer's way to taunt you for some reason. I'd watch myself, if I were you."

The rest of the trip was spent discussing possible enemies from Mark's past, connections to the military, and anything else that they thought could help the case. It felt good to have someone to act as a sounding board for him again. It was also nice to get a break from Quincy.

The night's sleep he got at the hotel in town was the best he'd had since this nightmare had begun.

11:01 a.m.
- Quincy, Pennsylvania -

Chief Kidd's office was a typical low budget one. The furnishings were meager, and the space limited. While it was true she did reside in the largest office in the building and it afforded a partial view of the Quincy Courthouse's expansive front lawn, the room was definitely cramped with more than two people in it. She had her office decorated with minimal clutter. Her desk was the largest piece of furniture in the room. It was a redwood desk, stained dark brown, with oak paneling and mahogany drawers. It had been a bitch to get it in the office, but the prior one was so worn out she'd been afraid it would fall apart while she was doing paperwork. Fortunately, it had waited to collapse until it was being moved out of her office. A round redwood end table with a tall antique vase on it occupied the corner to the left of her desk, and a planter with a bunch of magnolias in it was off to the right. The chair behind her desk was a comfortable plush one, and there were two small wooden chairs with a cushion tied to the seat in front. On the wall by her door was a compilation of certificates chronicling her life's achievements.

Currently the three large, rough looking FBI agents joining her in her office made it feel overcrowded. Sitting in front of her desk were Special Agents Dustin Hugo and Bradley Mouch, while the junior Special Agent, whose name she didn't yet know, stood unobtrusively to the right of her door, trying to not dislodge any of her wall hangings. Special Agent Hugo, who appeared to be in charge, was a tall, athletically built Hispanic man, with a full head of dark black hair and piercing brown eyes. His suit was standard issue FBI, but looked two sizes too small on him. Every time he moved, she was afraid his body would burst through the fabric. Hugo reminded her of a hot Latino weight lifter she had known while going to high school, and would probably be attractive if he didn't take life so seriously. He acted like someone needed to remove the corn cob someone had stuck up his ass years ago. His partner seemed to be the exact opposite. Mouch was about her height, and skinny. He had a blond crew cut and blue eyes, with high cheek bones and an Ichabod Crane looking nose. His suit was loosely fit and very comfortable looking. He seldom spoke, but seemed to be the less arrogant of the two.

"The FBI hasn't officially taken over yet, but I've been told to advise you that the Director says if one more incident happens, your investigation will seriously be in jeopardy of becoming ours," Special Agent in Charge Hugo responded to her previously asked question.

"I can understand the Director's take on the situation, and respect the responsibility he's placed on my shoulders. Obviously the pressure to achieve results is high. What can I expect as a way of support for us here?" replied Kidd.

"We have a full team of agents at your disposal, including an analyst and several experienced tacticians for overall strategy planning. We would like to inconspicuously insert a few of our men into the community itself to help ensure the town's security, as well as help flush out the perpetrator. We believe the town's security has been in serious jeopardy as of late. And the Director requests a town curfew, among some other precautions, be put in place."

"Look I called you guys for the assist. I don't need the town's residents panicking. What you seem to be asking is for martial law to be implemented. While I agree things are bad, and the community is scared, I don't think a panic will help. In fact it will only create more chaos," Kidd's voice rose in concern.

"This town has possibly the worst serial killer under investigation in the last century, killing its people. You've had upwards to one hundred deaths in two weeks. It may make people uncomfortable, but security should be your first priority," Hugo replied accusingly.

Interrupting his partner, Mouch said delicately, "Chief Kidd, we realize the strain this community has been under. We do not mean to downplay that struggle at all, nor do we think you've handled the situation poorly. Our concern is the safety of your community. That is our first priority."

Glancing at both of their faces, and then turning her chair around to face the window, Kidd contemplated the situation and wondered if St. James had been right. Looking out of the second story window, she could see families walking down streets and cars driving throughout town. This was her home, and apparently in order to defend it she was going to have to make a deal with the FBI. Sometimes when you wanted to trap the devil, you had to bed the dragon.

Turning back to the FBI agents, she clasped her hands together in front of her, and said, "What other precautions are we talking about?"

CHAPTER 22

REHEARSAL

Tuesday, May 23
1:12 p.m.

Mark stood in the kitchen while Mr. and Mrs. Benson sat at the kitchen table and ate their lunch. Kiara was in the other room preparing for her day at her high school's graduation rehearsal. Apparently, she hadn't been able to see any of her classmates since the death of Daniel, and she was nervous. Being in her shoes, he would've been upset as well.

"So, Mark, we still haven't finalized your bill for protecting our daughter," Mr. Benson said.

"I told you at the hospital when I first took the case, it's not a big deal to me. I know your family is on a tight income and obviously I'm not in need of money. My normal fees are $10.50 an hour or $75.00 per day, but under the circumstances I'll work something out with you after we get through this mess. I don't want you to worry about the bill."

"I can't allow that." Getting up from his chair, Mr. Benson walked over and handed him an envelope he'd taken from his back pocket, "I know it's not much, but you've been here. Not many people would have done what you've done to protect our daughter. Thank you."

Slipping the envelope into the inside pocket of his jacket, he commented, "It wasn't necessary, but thank you."

Kiara walked around the corner at that time and went to sit with her parents. Everyone was silent as she grabbed a BLT, handful of chips, and poured a glass of milk, then began eating. She wasn't his daughter, but she could read the same conflicting emotions on the Bensons' faces that would have been on his. Fear, pride, happiness, worry, and sadness. It was all there.

"Okay, honey, your father and I discussed it and we decided to go with Mark's recommendation. You can leave the house with supervision while the sun is up and visit with your friends tomorrow during the game. Mark has assured us that with the additional FBI security detail in town the risk of anything happening to you is minimal."

Kiara had a large, clown like smile on her face, and almost knocked her chair over as she got up, practically leaping over the table to hug her parents. She just kept repeating, "Thank you," then after a few minutes of this looked at him and said, with enthusiasm, "Thank you for this, Mr. St. James. Trust me, I know the risks and will be responsible."

"I do trust you, just go with your instincts like you did to survive originally, and you'll be fine," he replied, "I'll still be hanging around until this is over, so if you need anything or are worried let me know."

"I will, thank you for trying to make this difficult time in my life easier," she responded. "I'm gonna go text Carmaine."

Kiara began walking away, turning back, she snatched up her lunch plate and milk, then strolled out of the kitchen.

2:30 p.m.

Mark watched as the principal discussed with the seniors how everything at graduation would progress. Each of the students had a copy of the schedule and took their place where the principal told them to, as he directed the rehearsal for the next day. The high school auditorium where the rehearsal took place was a huge room which could hold about 1,000 people. There was a stage at the front and hundreds of comfortable, theater-style, chairs set in rows, with plenty of room for additional chairs to be brought in if needed. There weren't any additional chairs put out right now, because graduation was actually going to take place at the football field. It was supposed to be a beautiful day tomorrow, and with everything the town had gone through over the last two weeks, everyone wanted to make the best of it.

He could remember his own graduation at this very same high school 25 years ago. The principal hadn't changed much, just gotten older and balder. Principal Brent Stikler was 61 years old, had a thinning mop of white hair on top of his head, blue eyes, and a lot of wrinkles on his face. He wore his usual tan suit, and although he appeared feeble in nature, he was in fact a highly intelligent and intuitive man.

Mark's graduation had been held in this auditorium because of rain. It had been a spectacular event. He could still remember the valedictorian's speech, mainly because his best friend, Jon, had given it. Even now it seemed just like yesterday. It felt odd that 25 years ago he had been standing in this very room.

Interrupting his reverie, Mark heard the click clack of high heels on the auditorium's cement floor and smelled Rebecca's perfume as she walked up behind him and said "Thought I might find you here."

"Yeah, you caught me. Kiara's up there, had to keep an eye on things. Her parents still trust me more than anyone else. They thought since this is really her first time out since the memorial, I could be here to make her more comfortable. The three thuggish looking men standing randomly around the room are her FBI escorts."

"You don't seem too thrilled to see them. Still harboring ill feelings from before, huh?"

"It's hard not to when the bastards practically crucified me after I shot The Hangman."

"You know it wasn't anything personal, Mark. They just had to do their job. You killed the man, it didn't appear to be in self-defense. Even you said it was a reflexive move."

"Hey, I know. I see the scenes of that part of my life in slow motion almost every day. It still doesn't help me feel any better," he growled, angrily.

"I'm sorry. That's not why I came here. Please calm down."

"Sorry. I'm sorry, I'm just having a hard time still with the drive-in murders, and everything else."

"I know, that's actually one reason I'm here. I was hoping that we could have dinner tonight at my place. I thought it might give you some time to take your mind off of things."

"Sure. I'd like that."

"By the way, how did your trip to Baltimore go?"

"Surprisingly well. I slept a restful night for the first time in months last night. I think my friend down there may have helped me break this case wide open."

"Really, why do you say that?"

"I don't know. There has been something about this killer that's been itching at the back of my mind ever since talking to Major Brusskin. I can't quite pin it down though."

"Well, maybe a relaxing dinner with me will help."

"Yeah, maybe."

"So, see you around six."

"I'll be there."

Rebecca squeezed his shoulder and walked away. He still didn't know what to do about her. His feelings were so conflicted. Oh well, hopefully with time he'd sort it all out, or it would take care of itself.

Chapter 23

Surprises

Tuesday, May 23
6:09 p.m.

The door opened in front of him, and Rebecca ushered his soaking body in out of the rain. The weather had turned sour. It had begun pouring rain about an hour ago. It seemed the gods didn't want their little town of Quincy to enjoy life. The graduation had been postponed due to weather. Kiara hadn't been very happy when he'd left her house a short while ago.

Making a quick stop at home to clean up, he arrived for dinner with Rebecca shortly after six. Entering her home, multiple aromas teased at his senses. Her house smelled absolutely delicious. Taking from her hand the towel that she had grabbed, ducking into her bathroom on the way to the dining room, he began toweling himself dry. Following her into the kitchen from the dining room, he never even noticed how familiar he was with her house.

He came here two or three times a month for dinner. It helped him maintain his sanity. She had truly made a home for herself here. There were dozens of shelves - big and small - lining her walls with hundreds of porcelain figurines. Angels, frogs, deer, boys playing soccer, girls in dancing dresses, a church choir, an old man fishing and another knitting mittens. The list went on and on: if it had been made, she collected it. He'd asked her once where she'd found so many figurines and she just replied "oh, here and there," but she had a story for each one. She'd been collecting them since she was a little girl. Even then, she had had a keen imagination.

Her house had a very homey feel to it. The living room had a fireplace with a forty-inch plasma TV hanging above the fireplace. She'd gotten the wiring for cable and electricity specifically installed so the cables couldn't be seen outside the TV. There was a large sofa in front of the fireplace, with a homemade blanket - made by her grandmother - lying on the back of it, end tables at both ends with colorful porcelain lamps on them, and pictures of family carefully placed around the lamps. A love seat sat on one side of the room beside the front window, and a rocking chair, where Rebecca normally read books, on the other side, in the far corner. The floor was linoleum, so she had placed a large, elaborately designed, Persian throw rug in the center of it. The sofa and end tables consumed a portion of the rug near the entryway. Besides the shelves of figurines, the walls held pictures of various moments in her life.

As they passed through the dining room, he briefly noticed a new edition to her figurine collection on a shelf near the kitchen. She had made her kitchen into a kitchen/dining room when she moved in, so there wasn't actually a clear difference between the two, unless of course you were Rebecca or knew her well enough to tell the difference. The first floor of her house had a living room, bathroom, and the kitchen/dining room to the right, as you entered, and a closet to the left leading to the staircase which led upstairs. Toward the back of the first floor, there was a laundry room, which had a door in it leading to the driveway, as well as a door which led to the basement. Her house was of moderate size, and could actually serve as the home for a four-person family quite comfortably. Even though she told people she never felt lonely in this house, he knew differently. He knew she'd bought it so she could begin a family here, though she'd never admit it.

Finding the origin of the delicious aroma he'd smelled upon entering, he heard - and felt - his stomach rumble in anticipation. She had made chicken tortellini with homemade garlic bread-sticks, sautéed vegetables, and a fresh garden salad. Grabbing two plates, some silverware, and glasses, he took them to her dining room table and began setting it. As he did so, he asked "So, how was your day?"

"Okay, we had a shortage of doctors because of a late spring flu epidemic. I had to fill in, so I was in the ER when a child who had been abused by his father came in. Apparently, it had been happening for years, but this time he'd broken several of his son's ribs. It amazes me how even now people still do horrible things to each other."

"Yeah, you'd think in light of this serial killer terrorizing our town, people would wake up, but they don't," he replied, with a hint of exasperation in his tone.

The conversation continued as he finished setting the table and she brought the meal in. Compliments were never needed: as always Rebecca's cooking was excellent. He hadn't realized how hungry he'd been until he'd reached for his third helping and a fifth breadstick, but then again, he hadn't eaten much lately because of everything that had been going on. Afterwards, he helped her clean up, as he was accustomed to doing.

About eight o'clock, they sat down on the sofa and she put a movie in that she'd bought at the thrift store in town. It was The Manchurian Candidate, a remake of a classic Frank Sinatra film. Rebecca leaned against him, in the naturally comfortable way she always did when they had evenings like this. Even though he knew he'd disappoint her again when he left later, he always allowed her to do this because he couldn't stand to see her un-happy. Which was ironic, because he knew that when he left, she would be just that.

10:42 p.m.

As always, leaving Rebecca's house was difficult, but he still couldn't get himself to stay all night there. Especially now, when all these old memories were being dredged up. Instead of driving home immediately, he decided to stop at the office to check mail and messages, since he hadn't been there much lately. He knew it was late, but any time a free moment came up he tried to make good use of it. Pulling up in front of the two-story office building, he got out and left the car running since he didn't expect to be here for long.

Unlocking the door and walking up a flight of stairs to his second-floor office, he entered and immediately noticed his answering machine light blinking. Bending over he picked up some junk mail, bills, and advertisements the mailman had dropped in his door over the last few days and then walked over to his desk. Sitting down he pressed the play button to listen to the messages and turned on his computer. The first message was from the Major telling him he enjoyed their weekend visit and to come down anytime, then there were a couple of messages from prospective clients, and the final one was from David Nixxon, inquiring about his offer of coffee and letting him know he would only be in town for a few more days.

Finishing up with his e-mails, he saved the final messages and grabbed the mail on his way out. Locking up the building, he got into his car and drove home. It wasn't a long drive, so 10 minutes later, he turned to pull into his driveway then slammed onto the brakes. A small animal appeared to be sleeping in the middle of his driveway, which wasn't right because most animals ran away when headlights flashed in front of them or at the sound of vehicles.

Getting out, he noticed that it appeared to be lying in a large oil spot on the ground, but then he realized the shadowy spot was the animal's own blood. Immediately he pulled his 9mm Glock out and surveyed the surroundings. Cautiously, he swept the perimeter of his house and found all the doors still locked, without any sign of entry. Putting his Glock away, he pulled out his phone, and for the first time approached the dead cat.

After pressing Kidd's speed dial number, he heard the extension ring several times, then her voice on the other end. Briefly he described the situation and told her he needed a forensic team.

Sitting in a car at the end of the block, The Surgeon watched and then laughed.

Chapter 24

Targeted

Tuesday, May 23
11:41 p.m.

Standing at the foot of his driveway, talking with Jon, who had decided to come over, he watched as the forensic team gathered evidence and took photos of the dead cat. Someone, presumably The Surgeon, had done a Colombian necktie to his neighbor's cat and put it in his driveway. There was no note or message included, but it was still very clear to him that he was being targeted. Somehow, even though he wasn't a lead investigator on the case or even part of the police force anymore, he had gained the attention of this sadistic killer. Was it possible the killer knew him personally? Was everything happening somehow connected to him? If so, it would drastically decrease the list of suspects. Absentmindedly listening to Jon, he heard him say, "Did you hear me? Earth to Mark. Hello."

"Yeah, I heard you. I was just thinking, why me? And to answer your question, yes, I do think someone is targeting me. I don't think it's a coincidence that there have been Hangman-style killings at all the crime scenes, and this just proves it."

Jon took some time to consider what he'd said as Mark continued to process the situation. Pulling out his phone, he dialed Rebecca's number and waited for her to pick up. Jon asked, "Who are you calling?"

"Rebecca--I have a hunch," then put a finger up to Jon, and said into the phone, "Yeah, it's me, Becky. Sorry for waking you. No, everything's okay, just dealing with a small situation here. No, I'll talk to you about it tomorrow. I need a favor. There is supposedly a patient at the hospital with Hodgkins disease. I need you to find out if this is true, then run a background check to see if they are related to a David Nixxon. I don't know, it's just a gut feeling. Yeah, thanks, talk to you tomorrow." Hanging up, he looked at Jon's inquiring face.

"What was that about?"

"About a week and a half ago, an ex-navy buddy of mine showed up. I haven't seen him in years and now, all of a sudden, he shows up claiming he has family here. Maybe it is just a coincidence, but I have a gut feeling and I don't like the convenience of it."

"You think this guy might be The Surgeon?" Jon asked, surprised.

"I don't know. I just don't like how he just happens to show up around the time all this started happening. I thought it would be a good idea to look into it. I wouldn't have thought about it, but I got a message from him at the office before coming home."

"You want me to tell Kidd and have him looked into as a potential threat?"

"No. It might be a wild goose chase, and with the FBI in town I don't want things to get complicated. Speaking of the devil," he pointed down the street as an unmarked FBI vehicle pulled up. Sighing, he rolled his eyes and said, "Great."

Mark watched as Special Asshole in Charge Hugo stepped out of his vehicle. He could see another agent sitting in the car in the overhead light's brief flash as Hugo opened and shut his door.

That man had been the lead investigator who'd tried to crucify him for killing The Hangman. He despised this man and could feel his hands clench into fists at his side. Apparently, Hugo had noticed as well, because he paused briefly at the end of the car before continuing to approach. He heard Jon whisper, "Take it easy."

"Nice to see you again, Mark. I'd say that I hope there aren't any hard feelings between us, but your body language already answers that question. You know I'm not your enemy."

"Could have fooled me. If you had had your way, I would be sitting in prison right now."

"Look I was just doing my job. You killed a man, Mark. Sure, he was a piece of shit murderer, but you can't take the law into your own hands. Besides, from our current situation, we can't guarantee you killed the right person."

"You son of a bitch," Mark suddenly felt Jon's restraining arms around him and saw Hugo backpedal a few steps, "You know Melvin Flores was The Hangman. We found trophies in his basement as well as the murder weapon. You're just pissed because Internal Affairs and your Director sided with me." Then trying to brush off Jon's restraining arms he said, "I'm fine, Jon. Trust me."

Suddenly, Hugo appeared to have become apologetic, and replied, "You're right, you embarrassed the shit out of me back then. But that was then and this is now. I'm sorry about what I said. It's obvious we need to figure out a way to work together."

"Fine! What did you want?"

"Just to find out what happened here, and ask if you needed anything. The Director told me to lend whatever help we could."

Surprisingly, the rest of the conversation went smoothly, and in the end, they agreed to keep in contact only when needed to for the case.

Wednesday, May 24
12:32 a.m.

The Surgeon wished he could hear what was being said, but it appeared that St. James had almost gotten into a fight with an FBI agent. He found the entire scene amusing. He had watched while St. James waited for the cops to arrive, witnessed the forensic team survey the scene, and was still watching now as he talked with the FBI. The Surgeon was a creative man. The scene he had created now was meant to enhance his need for adrenaline. He always felt a rush when he was at risk of being caught. In the end, he would kill St. James. He relished the thought of killing this man. It was St. James' fault his father had died, that he'd been left in Iraq, and consequently that he had almost been killed, as evidenced by the scar on his chest. The scar was a constant reminder of his dad's death and St. James' betrayal.

He could still remember the day his commander had told him about his father.

Iraq 1998

Working on a victim who had stepped on a land mine, he removed shrapnel from the man's chest while considering how to deal with the damage inflicted on the soldier's legs. There would be substantial scarring, and obviously this man would never walk again, even if his legs were somehow reattached. Suddenly his friend was by his side, telling him the Commander wanted him and he would take over. Nodding, he backed away, removed the latex gloves and facial mask, then tossed them into the bio-hazard bag.

Walking out from under the tent and into the desert heat never bothered him anymore. The inside of the tent was only slightly cooler than out here, but he took no notice. The desire to help people, when he joined the Navy's medical unit here, was what motivated him. Therefore, he endured the heat. He knew he was a good medic, but he still was unprepared for the carnage this war was causing.

Stepping into his Commander's tent, he stopped and saluted him then waited. "At ease, Sergeant. you may sit." The Commander's look was grave, which told him this wasn't going to be a pleasant conversation. "I've got bad news . . ."

Returning to the present, The Surgeon wiped a lone tear from his cheek, pointed his finger at St. James, in the shape of a gun, and smiled as he pulled the pretend trigger.

Chapter 25

Final Preparations

Wednesday, May 24
2:09 p.m.

Mark showed up at Kiara's house shortly before two. He wanted to talk to her about how graduation and the football game were going to go, as well as make sure she was still up for it. He found her in her room messaging her friends on Facebook. She appeared to be in a good mood again, and enthusiastic about tomorrow. The weather forecaster claimed the next two days were supposed to be sunny and in the low 60s, so the graduation was tentatively rescheduled for tomorrow afternoon.

"Hm-hmm," he mimicked clearing his throat.

Turning toward him, she said, "Oh, hey, Mr. St. James. Just give me one second," then resumed what she'd been typing on the computer.

Watching her, he wondered if this was how Molly would've been. After all Kiara had been through, she was still an innocent young girl. Sure, sometimes she was a mess, but lately she seemed to have gotten some spirit back. Finished typing, she faced him again and said, "Okay, what's up? You look like death frozen over."

"That bad, huh? I came by today to discuss some details about tomorrow. There was an incident last night and instead of talking to your parents about it, 'cause I have a feeling what would happen if I did, I decided to talk with you first. Now if you can't accept these new ground rules, I'll be forced to talk to them, so I need you to go along with me on this, okay?"

"What's going on, Mr. St. James? You saved my life at the memorial service. I'll do whatever you say."

"First, there's no need to be scared. No one else has died, but a very personal and disturbing message was sent to me last night, so I just want to make sure you are safe throughout tomorrow."

"Okay," she replied cautiously.

"Normally there would only be a couple of officers keeping you company, but tomorrow there will also be a couple of FBI agents at a distance, and I will be there for added security. Unfortunately, you are our only witness, and although we've lessened security ever since we announced that you had no information to provide on TV, I don't believe the killer is gonna leave you alone. I think, if nothing else, it comes down to his pride at allowing you to get away." Taking a deep breath, he could see he had begun to frighten her, so he changed his tactics. "Look, this is just my own speculation no one else thinks you are at risk, but I just want to be sure. I was hired to protect you and with such a publicized event happening, I want to cover all the bases."

"Well, whatever you think is best. You don't really think he would be stupid enough to try something tomorrow? I mean, practically the whole town is gonna be there."

"No one believes he will strike, however, given the highly public executions he's already done we want to be cautious. Anyway, besides the extra security, I wanted to ask you to try and limit the time you spend with your friends to 30 minutes. I'm gonna give you my emergency number too. If you need it, it will immediately page my cell and I will be there. Also, if you think you are gonna be longer, please let the officers know and they'll let me know. Can you agree to that?"

"Yeah. It sounds great. I would've liked more time with them and for this entire thing to be over by now, but I know it's for the best that we do it your way. Thanks for not telling my parents. They would have just made me stay home. They worry a lot about me."

"Just remember they only do it because they love you, Kiara. You're a good girl. Is there anything you need or want to talk about?"

"No, I mean, I still wake up from nightmares most nights, but that won't end anytime soon."

"Well, like I said your parents love you. Let them help you if you need it."

Walking away he headed to the living room to watch TV with Mike, the officer on duty. Standing in the entryway, he found Mike and Mr. Benson watching some action movie with Arnold Schwarzenegger in it. He still wasn't comfortable sitting in anyone's home, especially while on a job. Mark felt more prepared while standing and was used to standing from his time in the Navy. Mrs. Benson came by and offered him something to drink. He accepted an iced tea, and for the next two hours sipped on it while watching television.

8:04 p.m.

The Surgeon picked the lock in no time and entered the room. There was no need for stealth since the building was empty, so he just walked right in and got to work. Setting his bag on the ground, he quickly cataloged everything.

He was in a small apartment. To his left was a closet, and further in was an expansive living area. The furnishings were meager since no one currently lived here, but there was a small sofa, an armchair, and some miscellaneous weight lifting equipment which the last tenant had apparently left behind. At the back of the room was an empty book shelf with some loose-leaf advertisements on it, and a picture of an English carriage rolling down a street of 1600s-era London hung above it.

Walking through the main living area, he found a kitchen and bedroom at the back. There was a working refrigerator, stove and microwave in the kitchen. Checking the cabinets, he found some months-old cereal and cans of vegetables. He headed into the bedroom across the hall, where he found a queen size bed and end table. Looking in the bathroom, off the bedroom, he noticed yellowish toilet water, but nothing else remarkable.

He returned to the bag he'd left at the door and brought it into the bedroom. Placing it on the unmade bed, he pulled out the belt pouch that held his tools of trade and unrolled it at the bottom of the bed. Briefly glancing at all the tools to make sure they were all in their place, he removed a video camera with a portable stand and began setting it up in a corner of the room.

Technology was amazing today. With this simple camera he could relay the footage to any TV he wanted in a one-mile radius. All he had to do was turn on the satellite transmitter. With this recorder he could do anything and no one would know where he was. By the time he was done, he could safely move before they found him. People were so simple minded. The world was full of unique opportunities, but most people took them for granted. Of course, most individuals weren't trained to see what was right in front of them.

An hour later, he had the room ready for tomorrow's new and brief tenant. He just had one last thing to do and everything would be ready. Leaving the apartment he went to his borrowed vehicle, grabbed a large box, and strolled back into the building. Fifteen minutes later, he drove away.

11:16 p.m.

Sureshot dropped the final body into the bathroom tub and turned on the shower water. The cold shower water should delay the decomposition long enough for him to finish the job and leave. The family had been caught unaware when he'd first entered their apartment. He'd watched as first curiosity, then fear registered in the mother's eyes before he'd shot her when she answered the door. He had entered quietly, after shooting her in the head with the silenced pistol. He'd caught her before she could make a thud falling backward to the ground. Entering the living room he'd shot the father in the back of the head, brain matter flying onto the TV set, before he had known he was even there. Upon searching the apartment he'd shot the teenage daughter in the back of her head as well, as she left the bathroom after taking a shower. The towel around her body had come loose when she fell, revealing part of her slightly maturing breasts. It was sad, she would have been a good fuck later in life.

Now that the bodies were out of the way, he began cleaning up the blood with a bottle of bleach he'd found under the kitchen sink. He took his time, knowing it was always the details that got someone caught. He had to make the apartment appear empty in case someone stopped by. Luckily the bathroom was near the back, so no one should hear the water running if they happened to stop by or walk by the door.

When everything was clean, he looked around for some keys to the apartment and found a set hanging on the kitchen wall by the refrigerator. Checking the hallway before he left, he went downstairs to the vehicle he'd rented in Pittsburgh and grabbed his bag. Heading back to the apartment, he took the elevator up to the fifth floor this time. Randomness was also a way to ensure security during a job. It appeared the entire building was done for the night, because once again he never saw anyone.

Entering the apartment, he shut and locked the door, then put the chain in place. Walking into the living room, he set up his equipment. After all the preparations were done, he checked what channels were available on the TV and settled down on the couch to watch some late-night soft porn on HBO.

CHAPTER 26

GRADUATION

Thursday, May 25
12:30 p.m.

Kiara sat with her friends in the front row of the chairs that had been arranged on the Quincy High School's Football field. The ground was still slightly muddy in places, but out here on the ten-yard line, where the sun had dried everything up, it was nice. The temperature was about 68 degrees, and there was a hint of freshly mown grass on the mild wind. It had turned out to be a beautiful day.

Normally no one would be on this field until late afternoon, but then it had rained and her graduation had been moved to right before the game. That was okay with her though, because it allowed her more time out of the house and with her friends. Looking around, she could see the various officers and FBI agents that were here for security. It was almost creepy to see so many police at a graduation.

She looked behind her and saw Mr. St. James sitting with her parents seven rows back. It was a perfect vantage point for him to see her clearly. He'd been particularly protective this morning and so far today. It was almost sweet, if it hadn't also been slightly annoying. Her friends tried not to tease her about the overwhelming attention she was receiving, but they felt the situation was amusing. She had to admit, when she took a step back and truly looked at it, it did appear quite humorous. She almost felt like a princess or president's daughter.

The field was decorated with mortarboards lining it. In the center, the year 2005-06 was dusted onto the field and the principal had set up the stage on the 'home' end-zone. In all four corners of the field, bundles of graduation balloons were blowing slightly in the wind. Many observers sat in the bleachers to either side of the ceremony, camera flashes frequently sparking from the crowd. As for the students and their families, they took up half of the football field sitting in chairs lined up on the field.

A band started out the graduation ceremony with The Star-Spangled Banner, which everyone stood up for, followed by the Quincy High School song. After the song finished, they listened as several alumni from the last few years talked about dreams, goals, the future, and accomplishments. Each had a different message, but all of it could have been summed up —as "these are the best years of your life, be an achiever, and you can be anything you want with hard work." Forty minutes into the ceremony, Jeffery Donovan, the 2006 valedictorian, finally approached the podium. Kiara could hear several sighs from girls in the audience. Jeffery was the Q.H.S. senior running back, and would play later in the traditional end–of-year game. He was the most muscular football player at the school, with long blonde hair and blue-green eyes which constantly changed in the sunlight. Most of the girls thought he was the sexiest man alive, and worshipped the man as if his sweat were diamonds and he pissed gold. Rolling her eyes at the various comments she overheard, she sat back to listen to his speech.

The rest of the ceremony went by quickly and smoothly. Before she knew it, she found herself at the podium shaking hands with Principal Stikler, then waving at her parents and walking off stage. She went back to her seat and waited for her friends who were still in line. Finally, when everyone was finished, the band began playing "Till We Meet Again," and she found herself tossing her hat into the air with everyone else. She hugged her friends, then went to join her family.

Her mother was crying, while her father had a huge cheesy smile on his face. They both hugged her and said "Congratulations, honey," at the same time. They asked Mr. St. James to take pictures, and he did. There were pictures of her and her family, her and her friends—Clifford even snuck one in with just the two of them--and then her and a few of her favorite teachers. Everything was loud and exciting. Everyone seemed pumped up and enthusiastic as the ceremony transitioned smoothly into the graduation party held at the other end of the field.

The school had provided meat and cheese trays, cookies, cakes, pies, and an assortment of snacks which must have cost them a good portion of their budget. There was also an assortment of iced punches - which had to be constantly monitored because of the heat and table bumping. She found herself smiling and eating snacks with her friends. It seemed like after everything that had happened to her, things were right again; but then she thought she saw Daniel standing off in the crowd. It caused her to momentarily halt, and she immediately ran over and turned him around only to find someone else. Almost immediately Mr. St. James was at her side, concern on his face.

"Are you okay?" he asked.

"Yeah, just thought he was someone else. No big deal."

"You're crying, Kiara," he told her.

She hadn't even felt the tears on her face. Rubbing them away, she turned and walked away. He followed, but kept his distance, sensing she needed space. Carmaine came over, and she found herself hugging her tightly. A few minutes later she saw her parents talking to Mr. St. James, who appeared to be consoling them. Once again, she found herself in his debt for saving her from needless embarrassment. The rest of the party went by uneventfully.

1:45 p.m.

Sureshot sat in a chair near the living room window, eating a grilled cheese sandwich he'd made on the stove. He watched through his high-powered binoculars as the graduation progressed from ceremony to party and felt the adrenaline begin to course through his body in anticipation as the coming cataclysmic event approached. Everyone looked so cute in their graduation gowns and dress outfits. As he put down the binoculars, everyone shrank back to looking like ants from a block and a half away. He took a drink of Coca Cola.

Returning his attention to the ceremony on the field, he looked at his watch and said to himself, "What the hell, I've got time." Taking all his clothes off, he sat at the window and began jerking on his hard cock as he imagined killing several people in his view.

3:18 p.m.

Parking the car outside the building, The Surgeon checked the streets, then got out of the car and opened the back door. Carefully lifting the body out of the vehicle, he quickly walked over to the doorway and entered the door he had left unlocked last night. Taking the stairs two at a time, he stopped in front of the apartment door and set the body down. Picking the lock quickly once again, he picked the body back up and entered the apartment.

Chapter 27

Non-Traditional Football

Thursday, May 25
4:46 p.m.

The final game of the year, which was the ninth and tenth graders versus the eleventh and twelfth had been under way for about 40 minutes now. Surprisingly, the underdogs - new recruits - were up by seven. Even with Jeffery running it in for two touchdowns, the score was 31-24. This game had been a town tradition for 42 years, and although it had been discouraged by several town people in light of the recent events the town council had decided with the extra security provided by FBI it would help improve town morale.

Mark sat near Kiara's family watching the game. He had just seen her walk off with her friends about ten minutes ago, so he was just here to keep an eye on the parents and enjoy the game for a little while. Kidd had agreed to place his two closest friends on the force, besides Jon, on Kiara's detail. She'd been kind of difficult at first, considering that almost every cop in the town had been called in to cover the event. Gary and Tom had practically been on the case from the start, which was one reason she had relented. They were good cops and very careful at what they did.

Sitting back, he began trying to connect the dots again, since his gut feeling hadn't panned out. Rebecca had called him at home this morning shortly before he'd left for Kiara's. She'd told him there were two patients being treated at the hospital for Hodgkins Disease, and yes, a David Nixxon had signed into the visitor's log several times for one of them. He'd thanked her, and after she explained that she hadn't been able to confirm anything except for what was in the sign-in log, he told her not to worry about it. He couldn't see The Surgeon taking that type of risk and being that thorough, so he was back to ground zero.

No matter how hard he looked at this case and all of the possible conclusions, he still couldn't get past the overwhelming evidence that he somehow knew this killer. First, there were the repetitive Hangman style killings. Of course, he couldn't look past the fact that in each case it represented a family member from his own horrible past. Then, the fake attempt on Kiara's life at the memorial service; that felt like a direct slap to his face. And finally, the dead cat from two nights ago. It was just way too personal for him to think otherwise. It made him feel totally powerless. The answer was right in front of his face, he knew it.

He looked at his watch and noticed it had been almost 25 minutes since Kiara left. He checked the battery strength and satellite reception of his cell. Both had full bars. His stomach was in tangles. It felt like the calm before the storm. These feelings reminded him of when he'd been in Iraq just before a firefight. He felt his anxiety levels rising, and a burst of adrenaline charged through his system. Suddenly, his body was on high alert. He looked around; the situation appeared fine. He saw several of-ficers and FBI agents patrolling the crowd. He visibly jumped when he heard his cell phone ring, and felt heat on his cheeks and neck as his face flushed in embarrassment. Looking at the caller I.D., then shrugging off his previous feelings, he took a few deep breaths and forced himself to relax. Obviously, he had worked himself up over nothing.

Answering the phone, he heard Rebecca's melodious, angelic voice on the other end. "Hey Mark, how's the game?"

"Good. The seniors just took the lead again. There's about ten minutes left in the game," he responded. "Where are you at?"

"Just left the hospital. Long day. Some of the doctors were still on leave."

"Sorry to hear that. Did you need something?"

"Yeah, look, something came up that I needed to run by you personally before I take it to Kidd."

"Okay, well I'll stop by your house after the game."

"No, I'm headed to your office now, it's closer to where you're at. I'll meet you there."

5:06 p.m.

Sureshot had spotted the target among the crowd of people a long time ago. He was currently waiting for the signal that had been discussed yesterday. He didn't know why The Surgeon had changed it yesterday-late in the game - but he didn't care. He had decided to remain naked as he killed tonight. There was a pot in front of his chair in case he busted a load as he shot people. The pot was just a precaution, because he occasionally had found out that he would ejaculate in the middle of his kills in the past.

Reaching beside him as he continued looking through his scope, he grabbed half of another sandwich and began eating it while he waited for the signal. Suddenly he tossed the sandwich aside and began his customary breathing action for steadiness. All he had to do was wait a couple more minutes and then the chaos would begin. He began a slow count to 100.

Finally, at the count of 62, he pulled the trigger.

5:09 p.m.

Mark never saw it coming. He was putting his phone away when suddenly he heard a pop and saw Mr. Benson's head explode. Mrs. Benson had time to begin a scream, and he barely had time to move before he saw the side of her head explode as she looked over at her husband. Blood and brain matter flew backwards onto other people in the crowd. That was all the time he had to witness what was happening around him, before he went into action.

He struggled through the panicked crowd, toward the underground tunnel entrance. Back in the late forties a storm tunnel had been dug under the schools for evacuating the children. In the sixties, when the football and baseball stadiums were built, the designers had had the wonderful idea of connecting all of them. Therefore, an underground tunnel now connected the schools to the fields, and the contractors had built the school locker rooms in the middle of each tunnel. Kiara and her friends were now in the girls' locker room that connected the high school and field.

As he tried to carefully press his way through the crowd, he heard babies crying, children screaming, and frantic yelling from all sides. Officers were trying to tell people to calm down and evacuate in an orderly fashion, but panic had filled the hearts of the people. He saw people being trampled, adults and children alike. Heads seemed to explode as people were shot, immediately causing others to turn the other way. The crowd was in chaos. He saw a girl of about six years of age fall down and barely managed to grab her and lift her into his arms before an elderly gentleman fell on her. The elderly gentleman was immediately trampled as another person was shot, causing the crowd to change direction again.

Finally reaching the stairway to the tunnels, he saw a traffic jam, since most of the people were escaping through them. Locating an officer, he passed the child off on her, and began his descent into the tunnels. Mark began yelling, "Kiara," at the top of his lungs every ten steps or so, but no one ever answered. He couldn't locate any of the FBI agents or Tom and Gary anywhere in the crowd. He hoped they had either evacuated the girls or were safely protecting them in the locker room. His heart raced with fear. He just knew he was too late. He knew he had royally screwed up. He knew he should have never let her go off on her own.

Reaching the locker room door, he found it blocked from the inside, which he immediately took as a good sign. The crowd was finally thinning out somewhat down here, so he could hear a little better. Pounding on the door, he yelled for Kiara again. He still didn't hear an answer. Taking a few steps back he slammed against the door and felt something shift, then the door opened grudgingly. The smell was automatic and overwhelming. It was at that moment that he knew his assessment moments ago had been wrong.

Slipping into the room, Mark found the carnage he had hoped he could protect Kiara from. He had failed his job.

CHAPTER 28

CHAOS & FAILURE

Thursday, May 25
5:26 p.m.

Upon entering the room, Mark found a heavy-set FBI agent had somehow been propped against the door. A bunch of rope had been tied around his body. He appeared to have fallen from somewhere above. His throat had been sliced clean through and hung loosely back from his neck. From the lack of blood in the doorway, he could only assume the agent had been killed elsewhere.

Walking further in, he pulled out his Glock just in case, though he didn't think he'd be needing it. Turning the corner around the first set of lockers, there was nothing to see, but the stench was stronger. He found her toward the middle of the room, spread out on a bench. Her arms were tied to the stool's far leg, and her legs to the nearest. From the raw marks around her ankles and wrists, it was obvious to him that The Surgeon hadn't taken the time to paralyze her. She was completely naked, her chest was bared open with the killers ritualistic y-incision cut into it.

He could see her ribs. Her heart and lungs were visible through them, as were as the rest of her organs. Sticking out of her belly button was her tongue.

Gary, Tom, the second FBI agent, and Kiara's three girlfriends were sitting up against the lockers on either side of the bench. Their throats had been cut, and all of their tongues laid in their laps. It was the second most devastating scene he'd ever seen in his life. Dropping to his knees, he took Kiara's feet in his hands and heard himself repeating, "I'm sorry," over and over again. That was how a Q.P.D. detective found him.

5:46 p.m.

Sureshot had just finished cleaning everything up when he heard the first sirens. Apparently, they were just now responding to the chaos he'd created. Overall, it had been an exhilarating night. While he hadn't needed the pot after all, he would have plenty of memories for later. He'd killed thirteen men, women, and children, not including the main targets.

He'd treasure for years to come the look on St. James' face when the first target had died. He had finished shooting everyone within the required 15 minutes. Afterwards, he finished the sandwich he had tossed aside and began his clean up. He started by getting dressed, then breaking down the sniper rifle and putting it away in its case. While doing so, he found himself chuckling every time he looked out the window and saw what appeared to be ants trying to rebuild a ruined nest at the field almost two blocks away.

Placing all of his equipment in the gym bag he'd brought up, he began cleaning all the dishes he'd used over the last half day he'd been in the apartment. He scoured all of them with bleach, using yellow scrub gloves on his hands. Putting all the dishes back, he then bleached the few things in the apartment he had touched without wearing gloves, as well as a few other things. He checked the couch for any hairs he may have shed throughout the night, and then grabbed his bag and walked out of the apartment.

Shortly before six o'clock he had completed his job, and no one had seen him come or go.

7:52 p.m.

Mark stood on the far side of the room near Jon and Kidd. Although the room was overcrowded with forensic, Q.P.D. officers, and FBI agents, he couldn't convince himself to leave yet. He knew he was only punishing himself by staying, but he had to see it through. He owed that much to Kiara and her family.

Neither Jon nor Kidd said a word; they just stood by his side, acting as emotional support, and glanced at him occasionally. It had been a couple of hours since they'd found him bawling at Kiara's feet, mumbling about how sorry he was. Jon was here because he was the only one who could pull him away.

For once no one bothered him with questions. Hugo and Stintz kept their distance. For the most part everyone was solemn. What had happened here today was unbelievable and would change this town forever. He noticed Rebecca hadn't been in here yet, but assumed since there were plenty of bodies everywhere, she was around. Staring into space as they repeatedly photographed everything, he unconsciously thought it was a invasion of the victims' privacy. Kiara's body was still naked, although in between photographs they replaced the blanket which draped over her. He felt like he'd betrayed her even in death.

When he finally noticed everyone begin to clean up and one of the coroners arrive to remove the bodies, he began absent-mindedly wandering out of the room. He headed in the direction of the football field and briefly took notice of the broken benches from falls. There was blood everywhere. It looked like the field had been drenched in it. He could see painted body signs on the ground, positioning where people had died, and evidence markers strewn around the place.

Looking around, he still saw no sign of Rebecca, so he decided to go back to the locker room so he could ask Kidd about it. Turning back, he almost ran right into Jon, and Kidd wasn't far behind him. He guessed they had followed him out here. Looking at Kidd he asked, "Where's Rebecca?"

"No one knows. She was paged an hour ago, and I've tried her several times, but it keeps going to voice mail."

His bowels clenched rapidly inside of him. He could feel his body go rigid. He heard himself say, "So no one's heard from here since she left the hospital, and called me."

Jon said, "She called you, when was that?"

But it was too late, something clicked in his head and he was already running across the football field. He heard Jon and Kidd yelling behind him, Jon sounded nearer than Kidd. Mark sprinted, faster than he ever had, toward the high school parking lot. Tearing the car door open and jumping in without any real memory of doing so, he briefly noticed Jon jumping out of the way, as he sped past him.

The ride to his office was very short; it felt like only a few heartbeats had elapsed since he'd left the field. Getting out, he stopped as he saw a car he didn't recognize, coming from the opposite direction, pull to a stop in front of his. Swiftly taking his Glock out, he glimpsed Nixxon climbing out of the car, then jump and immediately put his hands in the air when he saw Mark's gun drawn.

Nixxon asked, nervously, "What's with the gun, man? I'm unarmed."

Relaxing slightly, he replied, "What are you doing here, Nixxon?"

"I just finished a visit with my uncle and decided to stop by to see if you were here before I went back home for a while. My wife called and told me my son had gotten sick." When he saw that Mark had begun to lower his weapon he lowered his hands, "So what's going on? Why are you so jumpy?"

"Haven't you heard about what's happened over the last couple of hours?"

"Yeah, but I didn't know you had anything to do with it."

"My clients were killed tonight, and now my friend Rebecca—the town's medical examiner—is missing. The last time I talked to her, almost three hours ago, she told me to meet her here."

"You think something might be wrong. I can back you up, if you want. I don't have a weapon or anything, but another set of eyes could help."

Assessing the situation, Mark decided he probably shouldn't have come here alone. Accepting Nixxon's help, he went to the building, unlocked the front door and cautiously entered. Nixxon covered his back, since he held the only weapon they had between them, and they cleared the first floor quickly.

Heading up the stairs, Mark checked all visible angles, then quietly took the steps two at a time. Checking the door handle on the apartment across from his office, he found it locked. Deciding to check it last, since there was no real reason Rebecca would be in there and the door was locked, he walked across the hall to his office.

All was quiet, as he checked the door handle and found it locked as well. He didn't think Rebecca was here, since she wouldn't lock the door behind her after entering. As he unlocked the door, he said, just in case, "Rebecca, are you here?"

The lights were off in his office when he swung the door open, so he could clearly see the bright light coming off a TV sitting on the center of his desk. Walking closer, he saw footage of Rebecca struggling, tied up in a bed, with tape across her mouth, and heard himself say, "What the fuck?" right before everything went black.

Chapter 29

Revelations

Thursday, May 25
8:42 p.m.

Waking up to his face being slapped wasn't new to him; Mark just hadn't think he'd experience it again after returning home from Iraq. As he returned to consciousness, everything came back to him, and when he tried to get up he felt his hands being restrained behind his back. He heard Nixxon say, "Now isn't this fun," then heard the man chuckle and looked up into Nixxon's sneering face just as he spit into his eyes.

"So, you are The Surgeon. I knew I should have gone with my gut."

"Yeah, I heard you were getting close to figuring it out. You sometimes are just too lucky for your own good."

Sighing he asked, "What happened to you, Nixxon?"

"Well, let's see, the Navy trained me to be a healer. I put all my skills toward helping people--but they still died, so I decided, fuck it."

"Of course, they did, Nixxon. We were in the middle of a war. That doesn't explain why you're doing this."

"Why I'm doing this to you? Why I became The Surgeon persona? Or all of the above?"

"Let's just start simple. Why are you killing people in my town?"

"Simple, money. I was paid to do a mission, and so I did."

"Who's paying you to kill people?"

"All in good time, St. James, all in good time. You know, it's funny watching you squirm like this. All the times you forced me to do pushups or spit in my face while in basic training. Did you really think I could forgive you for singling me out just because you claimed I had the most potential?" Nixxon glared at him. "You were an asshole. You were tough. What happened to all your spirit, St. James? Oh, that's right, someone went and offed your family, so now you're nothing but a sensitive and pathetic has-been."

Instead of responding, Mark just sat there and observed. Considering his options, he knew he really only had one. It was the ace up his sleeve. Nixxon said, "What, no response?" as he got up from the chair he'd been sitting in and walked over to the desk. Turning the TV to face them and picking up an unusual looking pistol he returned to the chair in front of Mark. "You see, her, Mark. She's here because you involved her in identifying me, but then I saw the look in your eyes when you thought she was missing and I realized something new. When it hit me I thought, isn't this great? He took someone I loved and now I finally get the chance to do the same. You do love her, don't you?"

"I don't know what you're talking about on either account." But Mark knew he had sounded half-hearted, as he glanced at the screen and saw Rebecca's hopeless situation.

"Did you know you killed my father? Yeah, ya did. You probably don't even remember him, Michael Jacobs Nixxon. The best Navy S.E.A.L. in the nation."

Suddenly, everything made sense. Why it was so personal for Nixxon, and why he had chosen to keep killing in this town, instead of keeping to his normal M.O. "I didn't kill your father, David. And yes, I do remember him. He was the finest S.E.A.L. I knew. He was the best C.O. I had ever had."

"Don't you talk about him. You don't get to talk about him like that," he yelled.

Mark had to keep him talking. He didn't know how long he'd been out, but he didn't think it would take long for Jon to realize something was wrong. Especially after he'd run off like that. "I'm sorry about your dad, I really am. Listen, when you graduated basic training, you told me you were becoming a medic instead of a S.E.A.L., to honor your mother. How does any of this honor her?"

Instead of calming down, David became even more visibly agitated, then got up and began pacing. "You really have no clue, do you? The Navy killed both of my parents. A drunk doctor killed my mother in the middle of surgery. Then they covered it up to save their own asses. On a mission for the government, you got my dad killed and left him behind. Did ya think I could let them or you get away with it? The United States military has a don't ask, don't tell policy—based on a need-to-know basis. They commit heinous crimes in the name of national security, then blame it on Arabs or whatever nationality is convenient at the time." Nixxon's voice rose steadily as he talked, and Mark knew he was reaching his breaking point. He had to make his move soon. Falling back on his military training, he focused entirely on maintaining smooth facial expressions, and tried to not make any unnecessary body movements that would give himself away. He popped his thumb out of its joint, then slipped his hand out of the zipper cord cuff around his left wrist. In the meantime, Mark said, "Nixxon, that doesn't give you the right to take the law or the mission into your own hands. Think about your parents. They wouldn't want you doing this."

"Fuck you, St. James! You don't get to say what they did or didn't want for me. I enjoyed killing Kiara just to make you suffer, but nowhere near as much as I will when I kill your girlfriend, the same way, as I make you watch."

As Nixxon began to point the pistol at him and started to pull the trigger, Mark hurled his body at him from across the table as hard as he could.

Chapter 30

The Final Act

Thursday, May 25
9:10 p.m.

Rebecca could hear screaming coming from the other room. She didn't know what was going on, but she didn't think she had much time left. Struggling, she tried every trick she knew about the human body to try and get out of the restraints holding her to the bed. She'd tried to relax her muscles first, and then moved on to double joints, but that was hours ago.

She was at her wits' end. Fear was beginning to paralyze her. She knew she couldn't give in to the panic. She'd woken up tied to this bed several hours ago. A black man had then forced her to call Mark to feed him false information. She'd long ago soiled the bed, from fear and the lack of bathroom breaks. She was starving, and thought ironically that if she died tonight, her last meal would have been at the hospital cafeteria.

She didn't know for sure where she was, but she assumed she was at Mark's office building based on the phone call she'd made. Was that him who was yelling at someone? Was he yelling about her? Was he frustrated because he couldn't find her? Or was he with the black man, and in just as much trouble as her?

Oh, God, she didn't want to die. She found herself praying for help. Then she thought she heard someone struggling across the hall.

9:16 p.m.

Mark felt something fly by his head as he rammed into Nixxon, catching him off guard. He grabbed Nixxon's wrist, pushing the gun up and away from him as he thrust his knee into Nixxon's stomach. Mark smiled with satisfaction when he heard Nixxon grunt, exhaling air as he did so. The man quickly recovered, seizing Mark by the throat.

As they grappled back and forth both of them were looking for some advantage or leverage to incapacitate the other. Nixxon let go of the pistol, twisting his hand free of Mark's, then flipped Mark's body over his back. Jumping on top of Mark's chest, Nixxon began pummeling him in the face. As Mark attempted to block the incoming onslaught he wrapped his legs around Nixxon's waist, then twisted and threw him off of his body.

Quickly regaining their feet, they circled one another silently. Both of them were breathing heavily. Mark could feel blood leaking from his nose. Nixxon smiled as he threw a round house kick at Mark's ribs, smoothly switching his stance and kicking him in the head when Mark moved to block the attack. Mark stumbled backwards and almost tripped over the coffee table he'd just lunged across.

Seeking to gain the upper hand, Nixxon threw himself at Mark—but at the last minute, Mark kicked the coffee table into the air, almost losing his balance in the process. Nixxon crashed into the table, which shattered on impact. Picking up a piece of the end table, Mark moved away from him, gaining some much needed separation.

As he picked splinters out of his arm, Nixxon said, "You can't beat me. You trained me; I know all your moves, old man. Besides, I've always been the stronger one." He licked his lips as they curved upwards sadistically.

Considering his options, Mark decided it was time to show Nixxon some new moves. He knew he didn't have much time left anyway. Feinting toward the door to the hall, he watched as Nixxon moved to cut off his escape, then rushed him with the table leg raised high. Mark struck him square in the nose, and smiled as he heard a crunch and saw blood spray from it. Surprised by Mark's offensive move, Nixxon countered by twisting his arm up to deflect the next blow. Nixxon took hold of his arm, then quickly snapped his hand up. Mark felt his arm break and screamed in pain. Blood draining down his face and onto his chest, Nixxon followed up with a knee to Mark's abdomen, then slammed his elbow down on the back of his head.

Mark collapsed onto his broken arm, crying out in pain again. Nixxon laughed as he said in triumph, "I win, you lose," then kicked Mark in the face just as he'd reached his knees while trying to get back to his feet. Falling onto his back, Mark saw the strange pistol lying under the couch. Looking back at Nixxon, he recognized a smirk of victory cross Nixxon's face as he began searching the room for the gun.

Mark clambered backwards toward the couch and said, "What did you win, David? Nothing, because no matter how many people you kill it will never bring back your parents."

Quickly turning towards him, Nixxon snarled in rage, then threw his body at Mark. Quickly snatching up the pistol, Mark pointed and pulled the trigger. The last thing he felt before passing out was Nixxon's limp body falling on top of his own.

9:52 p.m.

It had gotten deathly quiet several minutes ago and Rebecca was scared. She didn't know what it meant, but she had the overwhelming feeling the silence wasn't a good thing. She suddenly felt tears falling down her cheeks as she prayed harder.

Chapter 31

Rescue

Thursday, May 25
10:27 p.m.

Rebecca felt her body jerk when she heard the apartment door open. She remained quiet and stopped sobbing as she heard heavy footsteps enter the apartment. She sighed in relief when she heard a familiar voice say, "Rebecca, are you here?" Since she couldn't speak, she did the next best thing and began banging the head board against the wall as she struggled in the bed.

Jon walked into the bedroom and cried in relief, "Thank God. We've been looking for you for hours." He moved to the bed, pulled his walkie-talkie from his belt, and said, "I've located Rebecca. She's across the hall, Kidd."

He peeled the tape carefully from her mouth, then grabbed a knife from the tools in the roll at the end of the bed and cut her loose. Setting the tool off to the side, so it was separate from the others, he helped her sit up.

"What's going on, Jon? Where's Mark?"

"He's across the hall. He's busted up pretty bad, but alive. The Surgeon is in custody. We found him lying on top of Mark, completely paralyzed. Apparently, Mark had given him a taste of his own medicine."

Ignoring her own discomfort, she quickly got up and ran across the hall. She found Mark on a stretcher with a splint on his arm and his eyes closed. Approaching the stretcher, she said, "Oh, Mark."

He opened his eyes at that and tried to smile. His handsome face looked as though he had just gone 12 rounds in a boxing ring. He whispered, "Becky, you're safe. I'm so glad."

She said, "Don't talk, just lie still." She felt tears stream down her face as she looked at him. What he had gone through to save her. She'd be thankful to him her entire life.

He reached up with his uninjured arm and wiped the tears from her face, then said, "I was so afraid for you. Don't cry, you're okay now. And I'll survive, too." He then fell into unconsciousness for the third time.

She looked up at Kidd, and smiled, "He's a strong and stubborn fool isn't he?"

"Yes, he is. But this town owes him a great debt," Kidd replied.

Rebecca nodded and then walked with Mark as the paramedics rolled him toward the stairway and peace.

Saturday, May 27
11:11 a.m.

Mark woke up and looked round the room. He realized he was lying in a hospital bed, and then remembered everything that had happened. At that exact moment he saw an angel walk through the doorway. Rebecca smiled as she came to his bedside, took his good hand into hers, and said, "Hi."

"Hi, how are you?"

"Alive, thanks to you."

"What day is it?"

"Saturday."

"I've been out that long, huh? Is it over?"

"Yeah, it's over. David Nixxon is in the hospital. Right now, he's on the sixth floor under FBI surveillance. Hugo told me to send his regards and to say 'thanks for not killing anyone this time'. Yeah, I know, what an asshole."

"He's still alive? But I shot him."

"You shot him with a modified tranquilizer gun, Mark. David is completely paralyzed. The lab analyzed the fluid and found a highly advanced synthetic spider venom. Apparently, the man had developed an experimental black widow venom which he had managed to weaponize. That's how he paralyzed his victims before killing them"

"He always was a smart young man,"

"Well, I guess he was too smart for his own good, now that he's the one who can't move anymore," then she laughed. "Serves the bastard right."

Mark laughed, and then groaned as he felt his ribs shoot sharp pain up his sides. Rebecca made a concerned face, then pushed the nurses' call button and sat down in the chair beside his bed.

A nurse walked in, and Rebecca told her to get him some pain killers. The nurse came back in a few moments and put a shot of morphine into Mark's I.V.

After the nurse left, Rebecca leaned forward, grabbed Mark's hand, kissed it, and said, "I thought I'd lost you."

Smiling, he reached up, grabbed her head, pulled it to his, and kissed her. Afterwards, he said, "I'm not going anywhere."

EPILOGUE

NEW BEGINNINGS

Monday, June 19
10:06 p.m.

Mark sat on Rebecca's couch. She was lying against him, and he twirled her hair in his fingers. His left arm was still healing from the fracture and hung at his side in a sling. They had just finished watching "City of Angels," and had turned on the 10 o'clock news. He sat quietly, holding her in his arms, thankful to be alive.

He had decided to sleep at her house, and in her bed, for the first time. He was taking it slowly, because at times memories of Susan still invaded his thoughts, but he knew now he wasn't disgracing her memory.

It felt good holding Rebecca in his arms. He leaned down and kissed her forehead, and she cuddled closer to him. It seemed she was constantly holding his right hand. As she reached for it again, he reflected on the accidental injury which had saved their lives almost a month ago.

He'd gotten it five years ago during a training exercise at Annapolis. It had been a routine exercise, training new recruits how to escape a vehicle in a firefight. During the exercise he'd been elected as the C.O. for the operation. Somehow, when jumping out of the vehicle he had managed to get his hand twisted in the seat belt and had been dragged 30 feet before the vehicle rolled to a stop. His entire hand had pins and plates in it because of the accident, but he'd also discovered he could pop any of his fingers out of place whenever he wanted to. It hurt like hell when he did it.

They watched as a special report came on the news. Pauline was standing outside of the Mayor's mansion, discussing how, in light of the horrific killings nearly a month past, Mayor Kendell Reid would be making a statement concerning fresh security policies he would be implementing. The screen then flipped to the mayor, standing at a podium on the front lawn.

He began by saying, "Hello, citizens of Quincy. It's been about a month since we were terrorized by a sadistic madman named David Nixxon, known as The Surgeon to the intelligence community. Over the last few weeks, you've heard many statements bringing you the story of the arrest of this killer, and our assurances that he would be brought to justice. Today, the FBI officially remanded him into custody and moved him to a detention facility in Pittsburgh as he awaits trial."

Glancing at his notes, he looked up and said, "This is the second time in just a few years our town has been invaded and terrorized by men like this. In light of this, effective immediately, I've instituted a new antiterrorism division at the Q.P.D. We want you to know this town will not continue to allow sufferings such as we've seen to continue."

Pausing for a drink of water, he looked back into the camera. The angle was perfect, and the camera clearly captured the hole that appeared in the center of his forehead as the back of his head exploded outward.

Acknowledgments

I would like to thank the following people for their technical assistance in writing this book. C.D. Lively, Cal Rich, Joel, Doug Stape, Amelia Rose, Dale Button, Melissa, Ogre, and Akiema. I would also like to thank my step-mom Diane for her financial support. A heartfelt thanks to all of those who've provided moral support and deserve an acknowledgment in this section: Albrandon, Aaron, Jeff, Russell, James, Chris, and Ken. To all those who provided suggestions, ideas and affirmations – Thanks! Finally, thank you to Cadmus Publishing for taking me into their family and beginning this journey with me. May it be long and successful.

To my readers, thanks for giving me an opportunity to entertain you. Writing this book was truly an achievement I'd never thought possible. It was an accomplishment years in the making. I've always wanted to write and now that my first book is completed, I'm looking forward to the rest. Hope you decide to continue with me in the future.

Finally, to all the readers of this book, if you purchased it on E-Book between February 2022 and its release to paperback, I apologize for the numerous spelling and grammar errors. I would like the reader to know this isn't a poor reflection on the work Cadmus Publishing did on my book. These errors are my fault and I take full responsibility for them. I would like to thank the editing staff at Cadmus Publishing for everything they've done to fix these issues. I thank the reader for your understanding.

ABOUT THE AUTHOR

Nicolae Andrews was born on an Army base in Arizona and spent his childhood in rural Pennsylvania near Pittsburgh. Growing up he enjoyed going to school, hanging out with his cousins playing war games and Atari, showing off his math skills to anyone who would pay attention, seeking to be the center of everyone's world, and his favorite past time – reading.

He purports to have read over 5,000 books so far and has had a dream to write his own novels since being a small boy. His favorite authors as a young man ranged from Judy Bloom to Dean Koontz and he has found inspiration for his own writing through authors such as Michael Crichton, John Sandford, Jon Land, Terry Brooks, and Robert Jordan.

At the age of 42, he lives in rural Kansas where he writes during his free time, watches movies, hangs out with friends and family, and continues his age-old pastime. Known among his brethren for both his wild comedic lifestyle and eccentric nicknames, such as McRuffkis and Stick, he tries to enjoy life to the fullest capacity he can. His only desire is to create and leave behind a legacy of laughter and a library of his own.